LOVE...WHATEVER THAT MEANS

Kathy Johnson

ISBN: 099722911X
ISBN 13: 9780997229110

This is a combination of characters
and stories,
true and imagined.

for Kimberly

With the invaluable encouragement of
Susan Huffman

Edited by
Sharon Roe

Cover by
Larry Scarborough

TABLE OF CONTENTS

THE WEDDING

It was Las Vegas and Christmastime.
It was Sin City and the birth of Jesus.
Santa was going to giveth, and the casinos were going to
taketh away.

Lourdes jiggled and tugged, multiple times, on the unmovable latch in the bathroom stall. With mingled emotions of frustration and resignation, she gave one final, angry jerk to the latch and with a flat hand pounded a few times on the door. Looking down and trying to convince herself, she grimaced.

It looked like clean tile.

With a shudder, she made the previously unimaginable choice to crawl underneath the stall door in her flowing, sleeveless, pearl-colored sundress.

Someone had gone for help, but given her state of mind she didn't care anymore. After carefully bending below the door, then standing to smooth out any wrinkles in her dress, she looked up at the other girls in the bathroom who were staring at her with pity and surprise.

Wordlessly, she washed her hands and joined Miguel, who was waiting for her in the lobby of the Las Vegas wedding chapel. He had been vacantly wandering through the front lobby where the streaming sunlight from the windows highlighted the swirling dust particles in the room.

"Did something happen in the bathroom?" Miguel asked, nodding toward the Ladies Room. "Someone came and got the manager and said that some girl was locked in the bathroom."

Lourdes made a muttery-mumbly sound, and her head bobbled 'no' as she sheepishly looked away - as though she was unaware of any commotion.

Her fingers nervously twirled her full, straight, brown hair with its natural golden highlights, her hazel eyes betrayed a hint of the fear of the unknown. She was not the fairy tale bride dressed in a Vera Wang wedding gown, the pretty sundress she was wearing was not sufficient warmth for the chill in the Las Vegas air.

Lourdes' natural fear of the opinions of others kept her from enjoying the fact that she was attractive. In her estimation, beauty contests were public versions of a girl's everyday experience. Girls line up in a row and turn around twice, so the judges can compare backsides to see who has the best bottom.

Today, she was too overwhelmed to worry about such matters as hair, dress and figure.

Miguel could best be described in holiday terms - a jolly, plump fellow. Typically, he was quick with a ready smile. His brown eyes were as shiny as his teeth were white. But today, his chubby cheeks were somber. He was wearing a peach, almost orange, colored shirt with a collar, making him look every bit like a cute tangerine. His faded blue jeans were still freshly pressed (even after a very long road trip to get here) with a sharp crease down the front.

The most striking element of this pair was the poster board drawing they were guarding. Drawn in black ink was a poorly-sketched portrait of Miguel's brother, Roy.

Neither Lourdes nor Miguel had a picture of Roy on their phones, and since Roy was the real intended groom, he must be present.

Although not artistic by nature, they had done their best to honor Roy so that Lourdes would have his face to look at as she walked down the aisle. His name lovingly written across the bottom, just in case there was any confusion.

A few other couples were waiting their turn; they mostly chatted among their own groups, noticed the poster board picture, but asked no questions. Lourdes overheard one of the couples, who it seemed had been living together for quite some time. Thinking it would be funny to announce a wedding in a Christmas letter, they had gone to *David's Bridal Shop*, where she perfectly fit into an off-the-rack gown, and spontaneously arranged a wedding for the sake of a Christmas card.

Lourdes wondered what her Christmas letter would sound like if she wrote one this year. The ones her aunt received were always such glowing reports of the successes from the previous year - as though no one had a care in the world or a misstep among them.

Maybe she could say something soppy like: "Greetings at Christmas! The most wonderful thing has happened! I have eloped! And as we think of Mary and Jesus this season, I am happy to tell you that I, also, find myself with child."

She frowned because the truth of her story was far more sordid than that.

Every advertiser knows that sex sells. It sells hamburgers, blue jeans, cars...

Girls also know that sex can sell relationships. It is the currency of the catch and the trouble that began Lourdes's story - a guy who used romance to get sex, and a girl who used sex to get acceptance and romance.

3

Her musing was interrupted as it was their turn to walk down the aisle, which was just as well, because today there were no clever devices or witty words to sugarcoat her situation.

Smiling, the woman in charge, who had already collected the fee, pointed out to Miguel where to stand while the music started.

Miguel went to the front of the chapel and dutifully held up the poster board which resembled Roy Rico only in the faintest of terms. Lourdes started her stroll down the aisle. Since there were only about ten rows of chairs, it was a short stroll. Each row had four or five chairs, some of the chairs had faded ribbons tied to them. It would be hard to tell their original color, but had probably started out as burgundy.

The traditional wedding music played softly from a CD at the front. Lourdes didn't look at the Justice of the Peace, or at Miguel, she looked only at her poster board groom.

Miguel's thoughts were not to look adoringly at the young woman becoming his bride. His thoughts were also with the poster board groom to which he held so firmly.

She heard the words, "Do you, Lourdes Anne Ferris, take Miguel Mario Rico . . ."

When it was Miguel's turn he followed suit answering, "Yes," at the appropriate time.

Miguel produced a ring, a handmade silver circle with some lined markings to give it a little flair. Roy made this ring in a high school art class - the only things in high school where Roy attained any skill were in making jewelry and ash trays.

Within a heartbeat, she heard the JP say, "Now you may kiss the bride."

She hadn't thought about the fact that weddings, even this wedding, end with a kiss. Lourdes instantly recalled being in second grade talking to her friend, Lisa, who said, "When I get married, I don't want to have to kiss a boy in front of all those people!" To which Lourdes had replied, "Well, have them say, 'Now you may shake hands with the bride.'"

The flashback was fitting as this would be the first time she ever kissed Miguel, and she wished for the handshake. This wasn't Miguel's idea of wedding perfection either. When he was in the second grade he thought he would get married in a car wash.

Timidly, they kissed their first kiss - a mere whisper of a kiss - for the briefest of moments.

Back in the lobby, Miguel asked, "What should we do with this?" as he held up the poster board.

Lourdes answered, "I guess, ummm, I really don't want to keep it." The previously prized poster board was unceremoniously left in the lobby trash bin.

Miguel had buried his brother, Roy, just a few days ago, and the goal of giving the baby the last name of Rico had been accomplished. Roy's last remaining hold on life on earth would have his name.

"Would you like something to eat?" asked Miguel. His last snack, some beef jerky from a gas station, happened about two hundred miles ago. Lourdes simply nodded. It was cold in Las Vegas - something unexpected for these two kids. Despite the chilly air, the sun was trying its best at shining making it feel warmer now than when they had entered the chapel. Not caring at all about the weather, they continued walking in search of food instead of getting back into Miguel's 1997 black Honda Accord.

The Las Vegas strip was filled with only a trickle of people. It was, after all, only two days until Christmas. The lights on the Strip blinked invitingly, and although the next week would bring the multitude of New Year's Eve party-goers, today the streets were nearly bare.

They followed their feet to the door of the *MGM Grand Casino*. They entered the huge, emerald-green colored building with its golden-yellow writing. Inappropriately dressed for the weather,

Lourdes was beginning to feel chilled, but once inside, she couldn't tell if it was day or night, hot or cold. The first sounds they heard were of slot machines dinging with the trumpet call of cash. Amidst the cacophony of sounds, they found their way to the *Studio Café* to grab a bite to eat before the drive home.

Home was Texas. They had driven straight through, a trip that took a good twenty-three hours, or maybe they were a bad twenty-three hours, depending on your zeal for road trips. They didn't stop for anything more than gas and to grab a quick snack. Lourdes thought Miguel had to be exhausted since he had done all of the driving. But in reality, he didn't feel exhausted. He felt nothing at all.

The *Studio Café* was basically empty. It was one o'clock, so there were a few people eating lunch but not many. The hostess greeted them at the podium, "Two?" she asked.

Miguel nodded and they followed the greeter. Although there were lots of empty tables, they were seated close to another couple who had already been served their meal. A moment later the waiter came, introduced himself, and asked if they would like something to drink. Miguel ordered a Coke, Lourdes a Sprite. They overly scoured the menu in a vain attempt to occupy their minds quickly deciding on what they always ordered, hamburgers.

Miguel's cell phone broke the silence between them, even though it wasn't an uncomfortable silence. He answered, "Hey . . . So what happened to Brandon? . . . Where was Dennis? . . . Did his mom find out? So, what did she do? . . . Grounded? Hmm . . . Did his girlfriend find out? . . . NO, man! You don't want to mess with these people. They'll shoot you over pot, man. Who knows what they'll do about coke. . . Yeah, seriously! . . . No, I put lots of fruit and vegetables in the fridge, but he still goes out for fast food . . . I don't know, he just won't eat healthy. Anyway, I got to go. Bye."

Lourdes listened to the one-sided conversation and asked, "Who was that?"

"Roy's friend. It doesn't matter now."

"Is he your friend, too?" she asked, wondering why if someone was on drugs Miguel was worried if they were eating healthy.

"Yeah," he mumbled while nodding his head. "I like him."

"You didn't tell him we got married. Does anyone know?"

"No." Then he asked her, "You tell?"

She had not. No one had seen her mother in years. The only trace of her mother left to her was a small, cobalt-blue medallion that supposedly came from her namesake, Lourdes, France, that her mom had given her when she was born. No one ever spoke of her dad. The only consistent people in her life were her Aunt Connie and Uncle John, who Lourdes had lived with (and their five children) most of her life.

Connie was a nice person - just solidly overwhelmed by life and all the trials that had come her way. Unfortunately, her face naturally looked stern and ill-tempered, her eyebrows were shaped like the St. Louis arches. When she was irritated, her right eyebrow would rise above the left one causing her to look positively sour. Lourdes had a good, but superficial, relationship with her.

Her Uncle John had taken in Lourdes somewhat begrudgingly, only because of the extra cost involved in having another mouth to feed and body to clothe, but his was not a soul that would turn away a child.

It was when Lourdes was fifteen years old that things became especially difficult with Uncle John.

Lourdes had tried to be helpful and self-sufficient around the house, an attitude which became a fiasco the day the cable wasn't working. Aunt Connie was out of town for the day taking her cousin to a dance recital. So, Lourdes took it upon her shoulders to call the cable company. The woman on the other end of the line kept asking the strangest questions and making her repeat her name and address again and again. Finally, the woman said that a repairman would be sent between two and six o'clock that afternoon.

The repairman arrived and discovered that her uncle had illegally hooked up the cable to someone else's line. He would now have to start paying for cable or not have it at all - either choice better than being charged with a crime.

Telling Uncle John what happened changed their relationship permanently. He had no cause to blame Lourdes, but he did blame her. Lourdes apologized repeatedly, and he smiled and went on. Still, there was always that nagging reminder (once a month to be exact) when the cable bill arrived.

Ever since Lourdes graduated from high school, she had been paying rent to her aunt and uncle. Aunt Connie claimed that *Dr. Phil* said it was a healthy thing for older kids to pay rent, but Lourdes already felt more like a tenant than a family member.

This all seemed normal to Lourdes, who as-of-yet lived an unexamined life.

She liked the people she worked with at the movie theatre, but there weren't any buddies she would hang around with there. Even high school felt a bit traumatic, she wasn't bullied - it was more like the other girls dismissed her with an unwelcome air.

No, there was no one to tell. Not really. Even so, Lourdes called her aunt and told her where she was without a mention of a wedding or a baby.

Fiddling with her new wedding ring, Lourdes wistfully asked Miguel, "What made you think to bring this?"

"I don't know. I saw it when I was throwing a few things together for the trip, and I thought it was a good use of it," he said with a shrug.

Sitting upright, Lourdes said, "I've heard of people who graduate from college 'dunking' their rings."

"Right. But you're not having a beer right now."

"Well, I could use this Sprite. And I could use the luck!" she said firmly.

"Okay. Here's to luck!" Miguel raised his Coke in a toast as Lourdes dropped her ring into the Sprite. A quick clink of the glasses, a hearty swig, Lourdes sputtered, coughed, and held her hands against her throat.

"I've . . . swallowed . . . the...stupid ring!" She grimaced, her hands still clutching her throat.

"WHAT?" Miguel half-way stood up, not knowing what to do.

"I guess it dropped on the ice, and, I don't know...what should I do?" she wailed.

Seeing she was still breathing, he wasn't sure there was anything to do. Before he could answer, the hamburgers arrived. The waiter, sensing this couple wasn't here for conversation, simply asked if there would be anything else. They both shook their heads 'no' and he left.

Periodically, Lourdes would continue to shake her head, maybe in response to unspoken thoughts - or maybe in disbelief as to what had happened to the wedding ring she had possessed for no more than an hour.

Miguel was just glad she hadn't choked to death.

The lack of conversation between the newlyweds meant the hamburgers were devoured in record time. The waiter was prompt with the bill and left it on the table while he cleared away some of the dirty plates. Miguel dug into his back pocket, pulled out his thin wallet, and left thirty dollars to cover the food and tip. He briefly thought how *McDonalds* would have been a cheaper choice for a burger, but seeing how this was, in essence, his wedding reception, he justified the added cost.

As Miguel looked at Lourdes, who continued to grip her throat, he mumbled something about how a wedding at a car wash was probably a better idea - grinning at a confused-looking Lourdes.

But it was the first time in several days he smiled.

THE TRIP

It was December twenty-third around three in the afternoon when the newlyweds started their trek back to Texas. The weather was clear and still very crisp. A quick stop for gas and they were on US Hwy 93 heading south to Kingman, Arizona, where they would then catch I-40. Lourdes spent most of her time gazing out the window at the passing landscape while Miguel drove, listening to sports talk radio.

After another stop for gas, a quick snack, and the day had slipped by. In the midnight darkness, the exhaustion they were both feeling began to settle in their bones. In Albuquerque, New Mexico, they found a small *Motel 6* with an available room.

Surprisingly, to both of them, they had a restful night's sleep. Neither of them commented on the fact that they slept fully-clothed in the same bed.

"A *Cracker Barrel!*" Lourdes enthusiastically shouted after they had been on the interstate only a few minutes. "Let's have a good breakfast before we start today. I don't think I've had any morning sickness, but I'm trying to keep food in my stomach, and yesterday I don't think I ate enough."

"Oh, okay, sure." Miguel said as he found the entrance to the parking lot. He pulled up to the familiar site of a *Cracker Barrel Restaurant* with lots of rocking chairs welcoming them to the long, front porch.

They were led to a table without waiting. After the waitress took their order, they sat nibbling on the biscuits and jelly. Lourdes, desperate to feel normal, said, "Last night I dreamed I was a cat trainer. I trained cats to be companions to rescued seals. Do you think there are people who really do that?"

"What? Train cats to be companions to seals rescued from the ocean?" asked an amused Miguel.

"Yeah. I mean, I don't know if I just imagined that - or if maybe I saw it on TV somewhere."

"Pretty sure that came right out of your imagination," he said with a grin.

After they had their fill of hash brown casserole, pancakes, eggs, and honey ham, Miguel paid the bill while Lourdes walked through the shop looking at all the beautifully decorated Christmas trees with their displays of toys and gifts. This was the first time it occurred to her that today was Christmas Eve.

"Did you find something you want?" Miguel asked when he found her.

"No, I just like to look. Hey, I want to use the restroom real quick, and then I'll be ready to go." Lourdes scuttled off to the Ladies Room, speedily returning having no desire to dawdle in a public restroom. After her experience getting stuck in the wedding chapel stall, she now felt a mild phobia about them.

Back in the car it was more of the same, Lourdes silently gazed at the passing landscape while Miguel drove. It wasn't until they were driving through Amarillo, pointing toward Oklahoma City that Lourdes gave Miguel a clue into what she had been thinking during her long silence.

Very deliberately, she turned toward him and said, "I've been thinking about the ring . . . and I've been worried about the baby.

11

I mean what if the ring got caught in the top of my stomach, and won't go down, and gets infected, and hurts the baby?"

She paused for breath then determinedly continued, "I know I can't have an x-ray because that would hurt the baby, but I want to know where the ring is, so, I've been thinking, my uncle has a friend who takes his metal detector out to find coins and lost stuff on the weekends – he found rings before. What if we get a metal detector, and do it over my stomach, and then we can know where the ring is?"

"Seriously?" Miguel's eyes widened, leaving traces of wrinkles on his forehead.

She nodded vigorously. "Yeah! I think it would work!"

"Where are we supposed to get a metal detector today? Don't you want to wait until we get home?"

"No, I don't wanna wait. I've been thinking about that, too. My uncle's friend bought his metal detector from a pawn shop. Let's just go to a pawn shop and use theirs for free."

Miguel cleared his throat, indicating he had never heard of such an odd idea. Using a non-insulting tone of voice, he calmly said, "I'm not even sure we can find a pawn shop open this late on Christmas Eve."

"We don't know until we try, right?"

It was close to four in the afternoon when they were outside of Oklahoma City. Miguel checked his phone and found *City Pawn*. Lourdes thought he hoped they would be closed.

They were not closed.

City Pawn, located in a strip shopping center, was a rectangular space that looked like a wide, cluttered hallway with florescent lighting. The glass door had a little bell announcing their arrival; they found stacks of CD's on the floor, a section of tools, lawn equipment, household goods, and musical instruments. The store had the look and feel of a disorganized garage sale.

The weather had turned from the clear, crisp Las Vegas air to a cloudy, heavy fog floating about fifty feet above the ground. The lack of sunlight coming from the front window made the unkempt business seem miserably drab.

The tall, skinny young man standing behind the counter looked quite uninterested if they made a purchase or not. "We're closing early today. Five o'clock," was all he said, and he continued to watch a small television with the state high school football championship game playing.

Miguel searched the walls for the metal detectors.

The walls were of made of long pieces of white slat boards where larger items were better displayed. They did not resemble stockings hung by the chimney with care. But, sure enough, there were four metal detectors.

"Lourdes," was all he said, and with a motion of his head, he pointed at the wall.

She tried to nonchalantly walk over to him while pretending to momentarily stop and examine a green vase.

Miguel took the first one off the wall. "Have you ever used one of these?" he asked Lourdes.

She shook her head.

He started punching buttons to see what would happen, but the detector remained silent. He put that one back. The next one was heavier and a little harder to lift, but it had a very clear 'on/off' button. Pushing the 'on' button, little blue lights began to flicker. "Okay. Ready?" he whispered sneakily.

Lourdes looked over at the guy who had greeted them. His head was bent down, now attentive to a text.

"Let's see how this works." He looked over at a wrench in the tool section, adding, "If this doesn't detect that big wrench, then it won't find a tiny ring in your belly." A moving swipe over the thick tool, and the detector began to chatter.

Satisfied, Miguel bent a little lower and with all the stealth of a chubby ninja, held the metal detector waist high, pointing at Lourdes. Looking left and right to make doubly certain no one was watching, he drew it closer to Lourdes. As he moved it down over her belly, it had a moment of chatter. When he got it further down her legs, the pings eventually stopped.

Slightly wide-eyed that this cockamamie plan might have worked, he laughed. "Well, I think there is something there. You don't have a pierced belly ring, do you?"

"Pffft, no," she scoffed. "Miguel, is it like in the top of my stomach - like it's stuck and hasn't moved, or is it at the bottom of my stomach - like it is moving through?"

"I'm not sure this is a finely-tuned surgical instrument, but I'll do it slower." Again, assuming his ninja pose, he slowly, but surely, started at the top of her tummy and ran it down toward her legs, careful to keep it a good six to eight inches away to avoid touching her. Again, there was just a little chatter, and as he moved it lower the sound intensified and then disappeared. "Lower. Definitely lower." He wanted to tell her this really didn't mean anything, but the relieved look on her face must have told him to keep that idea to himself.

"Okay?" he asked.

"Yes," she sighed, nodding her head up and down, "okay."

On the way past the oblivious young man, who was still texting, Miguel noticed the glass counter, where the little TV was sitting, had jewelry inside. He paused to look, finding a small silver ring, which was no more than narrow a band.

Lourdes stood at the door, barely within ear-shot of Miguel and the clerk. "How much for the ring?" Miguel asked.

"Wha? What did you say?" asked the kid, blinking back to the reality that he was at work.

"That silver ring. How much?" he asked pointing to the band.

"Twenty bucks."

Miguel pulled out his last twenty dollar bill and bought the ring. Back inside the car he gave it to Lourdes and said, "There's no sense in thinking you're going to keep THAT ring," pointing to her stomach, "so this should work."

The ring, a tad loose, easily slid on her finger.

Touched by his gesture, she said a bashful, "Thank you."

On the interstate again, Miguel listened to sports talk radio. Lourdes said, "It's Christmas Eve, would you mind if we listened to Christmas music for just half-an-hour? Then you could change it back."

Christmas music would not have been his first, second, or third choice, but he said since he had exercised control of the radio for the entire trip, it seemed only fair that for thirty minutes she should hear Christmas music on Christmas Eve.

Amy Grant was singing *"Tennessee Christmas"* while Lourdes lightly hummed along. "Miguel?" she said, as though his name was a question, "Do you really want to go home today?"

"Truthfully, no, not really." Miguel's expression looked as though he could have explained, but he chose not to.

"Let's go to Tennessee for a day or two," she said matter-of-factly, as though this had been the plan all along.

"What's in Tennessee?"

"Christmas, maybe - I don't know. Nothing really. It's just not home and I don't want to go home today."

The unspoken fact was that her Aunt Connie had once told a friend of Lourdes's that if she ever got pregnant, "she shouldn't bother coming home."

Lourdes had no sense of belonging, especially now that she found herself in this delicate condition. She was married, but only as a legality. A baby would not be a welcome bundle of joy, Aunt Connie and Uncle John would see this as another intrusion into their already stretched home and budget. She would either be kicked out of the house - or the constant tension and anger would drive her out. It was simply too hard to think very far into the future and if this could be put off even for another day, all the better.

"Lourdes, I can't afford it. I've spent all my money on this trip. We have to go home."

"I have a credit card with a five hundred dollar limit. We can use that. I'll pay for everything. Please," she began to shake her hands for emphasis, "what can it hurt? You don't really want to go back today, right? You don't have to work until after the first of the year, right? And it won't cost you a penny!"

There wasn't much time for a debate. Miguel was at the I-35 cut-off. They could go straight to Tennessee or take I-35 South to Texas.

He looked into her pleading eyes, and without a word, he nodded and drove straight ahead.

It was past Little Rock when Miguel changed the radio station and heard a local announcer talking about bad weather. A ferocious front coming from St. Louis held a thunderstorm. Behind the thunderstorm was an ice storm.

"We need to figure out a place to stay," Miguel said. "I sure don't want to get caught in an ice storm."

Before Lourdes could answer, he alarmingly said, "Hey! Did you see THAT?"

Up ahead there was something of a plume of rising dust being reflected by car lights. Squinting, Miguel yelped, "It's a tanker truck and I think it just flipped over!" Without a moment of hesitation, he pulled the car over, jumped out and ran toward the overturned tanker - disturbed dust or smoke was rising from its belly.

"Oh, God. Oh, God. Oh, God," she shrieked, now jolting out of the car so she could better watch Miguel. She stepped onto the grass, which was heavy with frost, crackling underneath her feet. "Oh, God. Oh, God," she moaned, continuing her perturbed prayer. "Miguel, COME BACK!" she yelled as she stood holding onto the opened car door.

By now several cars had stopped, as bystanders called 9-1-1. She lost sight of Miguel in the steady stream of help pouring from the stopping cars.

The wife of a fellow Good Samaritan saw Lourdes shivering and brought her a large overcoat to borrow while they waited.

"I don't know why he HAD to run over to that tanker!" Lourdes's voice sounded shrill on the night air. "What if it explodes? I mean is that dust or smoke? We need to figure out a place to stay tonight - not do something like THIS!" Her irritated overtones seemed exaggerated by her shivering.

"Darlin', it's Christmas Eve. You don't have a place to stay?" The southern-voiced woman oozed concern.

Lourdes's reply was garbled. "I'm sort of, well, on my honeymoon."

Shaking her head in sympathy, the lady said, "No wonder you're so frightened!" She turned on her heel, jaunted back to her car, saying, "I'll be right back."

Lourdes didn't want Miguel running toward an overturned tanker. She didn't want to have an ice storm approaching. And she certainly didn't want to be standing out here in the cold with some woman trying to make small talk.

A minute later, the middle-aged woman who was wearing black slacks with a heavy coat - and looked like she was either going to or coming from a Christmas party - returned. She said, "My friend has a Bed and Breakfast, it's not close to here, but she gave me this magazine so I could see her advertisement.

As I was thumbing through it, I noticed a few that aren't too far away. We're less than an hour from Memphis, and they have some around there. If you want, you can have this." She held out the travel magazine, which Lourdes accepted. "You don't want to be wandering around Memphis after dark with no place to stay."

The crowd around the tanker began to disperse. Relieved, Lourdes said, "Looks like he's coming back. Here's your coat. And, really, um, thanks." She handed the coat back to the woman and jumped back into the car with the magazine. She could make out Miguel's form as he trotted back.

"Miguel! Why did you do that? Never, ever, NEVER do something like that! You didn't know if that tanker was about to explode!" she continued animatedly, "I doubt it was full of milk!"

He simply responded, "I would want someone to do that for me."

Resigned, Lourdes shook her head. "Well, is the driver all right?"

"I think so. I never did see him. But we could talk to him. There were a couple of other guys there, and we had him turn off his diesel tank. They're going to stay until the highway patrol comes. I didn't see any reason for me to stay, too."

Finally, a sentiment she could agree with. Miguel put his blinker on, rejoining the line of travelling cars.

Holding up the travel magazine, Lourdes said, "A lady gave me this with the names of Bed & Breakfasts around here. Do you want me to call them? She said we're less than an hour from Memphis."

"Okay, but I don't want to go any farther than Memphis because of the ice storm. I don't care where we stay, but we stop there."

It was on the third call that she was able to find a place. "Okay, great. Oh, hey, you take credit cards, right?" Nodding her head she continued, "Now, how exactly do we get there?" Frantically, she scribbled the directions on the magazine cover. "Uh huh. Blinking light. Right, then straight. Curves a little. Driveway on the left. All right. We should be there in about forty-five minutes? Okay. Thank you so much!"

Feeling a little calmer, Lourdes said to Miguel, "It sounds easy enough - and the lady seems really nice. It's in a little town on the southwest side of Memphis. Just take the loop, I think I can guide us from there. Well, except I have such an awful sense of direction - maybe I should explain it to you before we get there."

Miguel seemed leery of the idea of a Bed and Breakfast but drove on, outpacing the storm.

Finding his way, Miguel took the loop, found the blinking light, and entered into the small community of Kingsville, Tennessee.

SAFEHAVEN BED AND
BREAKFAST

Safehaven Bed & Breakfast, a log home, was set back from the road by forty yards. Wild thick trees gave way to a clearing where the driveway widened into a parking pad with pea-sized rocks, four cars were already there when Miguel pulled in among them.

Nervously, Lourdes and Miguel got out of the car, shivering while they grabbed his backpack and her small overnight bag. The red, double front doors had fresh wreaths and smelled of Christmas. Miguel gave a solid knock, which was quickly answered. As the doors opened, the light from inside poured out, creating a dazzling contrast to the shadowy sky.

"Come in! Come in!" The woman greeting them was in her fifties, a happily aging hippie who looked like a calorie-satisfied Carole King. Her blue eyes were friendly, and her shoulder-length blonde hair fell in loose curls.

Her welcoming way removed their nervousness as she motioned them forward into the house.

Once inside, it took a moment for their eyes to adjust to the light. Absorbing her new surroundings, Lourdes marveled at the huge room with a high, vaulted ceiling, dark hardwood floors, with plenty of colorful rugs.

The log walls had been painted a soft pearl white.

On their left was a large, stone fireplace where a lighted Christmas wreath hung. The built-in twinkle lights were doing their best to compete with the glimmering fire in the fireplace. Several mismatched stockings hung from the mantle, each with a name hand-written on them. Standing beside the fireplace was a Christmas tree, beautifully decorated with an assortment of ornaments hand-made by children.

Lourdes had never seen anything so perfect, like something from *HGTV.* The fat chairs and cream-colored couches with fluffy pillows of different colors were arranged for conversation. The right side of the room had a long, narrow dining table with fourteen or fifteen wooden chairs of various sizes and colors. On the other side of the table was an archway that opened into the kitchen.

Quaint was the most appropriate word that occurred to Lourdes.

A whimsical charm filled this place.

Lourdes could hear the clatter of plates and pans being handled, looking through the archway she saw several people milling around. Their laughter was muffled.

The woman who answered the door said, "I'm Katie Barkley. Welcome to Safehaven! Helping a young couple stranded on Christmas Eve seems poetically perfect!" She gave an airy wave of her hands.

Merely a second later, a man, probably also in his fifties, walked up, stretched out his hand to greet his guests, and said, "Hello! I'm Tucker." His handshake was firm. His hair was fair with a twinge of gray, tied back into a pony tail. He was taller and stouter than Katie, although with her Christmas sweater her true size would have been a guess. Tucker's eyes were a happy brown, and he exuded the same bohemian welcome, putting both Lourdes and Miguel at ease.

"I'm glad you called when you did. I would have hated to have missed you! We're all going to a Christmas Eve program at church in a bit. First, we'll have a bite to eat. Are y'all hungry?" Katie looked from Lourdes to Miguel, smiling and waiting for an answer.

Overwhelmed in her new surroundings, Lourdes didn't realize at first that Katie had asked a question. Noticing Miguel was bobbing his head affirmatively, she joined with her own bobbling head. "Yeah. Thanks," she replied.

Lourdes and Miguel hadn't even thought about eating while fleeing the foul weather.

"Well then, let's see what the kitchen offers tonight!" Katie took their belongings, and laying them on the nearest couch, she walked toward the noise and the luscious smell of food.

Following Katie through the archway, Lourdes saw the kitchen counters were cluttered with various groceries and pots and pans. She wondered if it was always a busy place or if this was the result of holiday cooking.

Her eyes then fell upon one of the most beautiful things she had ever seen, a half-moon shaped window pane of stained glass of swirling greens, blues and yellows situated above a red door.

Already in the process of dipping-up dinner were several other people. Katie said, "Come meet my parents - Lourdes and Miguel - this is Cracker and Ginny Philpott."

Cracker's gray hair arranged itself like that of an absent-minded professor. His suspenders were patterned with snowmen and Christmas elves. Ginny wore a dark holiday sweater with dancing snowmen on the front and 'Merry Christmas' written in white script across the back. Her hair was the same shade of cottony-white as the writing on her sweater. They all smiled and nodded toward each other in greeting.

Pointing to another young couple, Katie said, "This is our daughter, Julie, and her husband, Luke. Their one-year-old son, Caleb, has already gone to bed." Julie and Luke smiled, but it was a haggard, tired smile.

Lourdes smiled at them with a slight nod of her head, and thought how lucky Julie was to have a family standing in the middle of a Christmas kitchen.

"Would you like some soup and sandwiches?" Ginny asked, while holding out a bowl from the cupboard.

Miguel didn't hesitate. "That'd be great!"

Emotions, unexpected and strong, whelmed over Lourdes. Now completely inundated with the amount of people and conversation, she asked where her room for the night might be to slip away and steady herself.

Encircled by this seemingly perfect family reminded her she was desperately alone.

By the time she returned, Miguel, now seated at the table, was eating heartily.

The steaming kettle of vegetable soup and grilled cheese sandwiches, chips and fruit had never looked so enticing. In spite of her melancholy, she was hungry and filled her plate.

The others had made their way back into the living room to sit around one end of the long table. Quickly joining them, grateful to be only visitors (not required to join the conversation) she sat down to quietly eat her dinner and fade into the background.

The older man, Cracker, looked as though he was counting heads around the table and asked, "Where's Tucker?"

Lourdes observed the man with the pony tail wasn't there.

"Oh, he went to check on the generator," answered Katie while she sipped and slurped the hot soup off her spoon. Then directing her words to Lourdes and Miguel added, "The nasty weather will probably mean our power goes out, but Tucker bartered for a used generator on *Craigslist,* and he wanted to make sure it was up and ready to go."

"I'm surprised he didn't already check on it," Cracker interjected.

Lourdes noticed this slightly slanting negative comment.

Katie seemed unfazed and answered, "He made his annual Christmas shopping trip into Memphis today and that threw him behind. I'm sure he would have preferred to have checked it already."

"Is that man still doing his Christmas shopping on Christmas Eve?" remarked Ginny, pushing her white hair back from her face.

She must have continued her explanation for Lourdes and Miguel's benefit because Katie said, "Tucker thinks the best time and place to do his Christmas shopping is at *Walgreens* on Christmas Eve."

After a pause, she gazed toward the Christmas tree and added, "He calls it his yearly, holiday Christmas tradition! His theory is that if they don't have it, then we probably don't want it. And actually, every year we get interesting gifts that we know he has put a lot of thought into. Last year he gave me bubble bath beads, plush slippers and a robe, along with about a dozen sugar cookie scented candles to set the mood for a perfect bath."

Lourdes winced, wondering how odd it would feel in the morning to be intruding on their exchange of Christmas presents. She hoped they would have their family festivities completed before she and Miguel came out for breakfast.

Ginny was clearing off her dishes when she asked the group, "Did I tell you we went to visit my Kansas City cousins last month? We walked into Loretta's house," and turning toward Lourdes and Miguel she said, "she's eighty now, and she was fretting over a mole that had changed. It was getting bigger by the day, but she didn't want to go to the doctor and hear bad news.

I lifted up the Band-Aid she'd put on top of it, and I said, 'Loretta! That's a tick! It's about to pop because you've been force-feeding it!'" Ginny chortled for a minute. "She was force-feeding a tick," she repeated, shaking her head with a laugh while walking into the kitchen.

Lourdes wanted to smile - but didn't. Although everyone seemed very nice, she wasn't sure if she was included enough to share a laugh.

"What's for dessert?" Cracker asked his daughter, as he sopped up the last bit of soup left in his bowl with his grilled cheese.

"Cookies." Katie got up and reached for a bag sitting on a nearby credenza.

Cracker pulled out an odd shaped cookie that resembled Abe Lincoln with his stove-top hat, and holding up the cookie as if it were show-and-tell said, "Well, would you look at that! Do you think that looks like Honest Abe?"

Katie's son-in-law, Luke, entered the conversation, saying, "You should sell that on *eBay*. Somebody might pay good money for it."

"Nah," Cracker said, popping the cookie into his mouth. "I prefer to put it into my Eat-bay. You know I carry my to-go box right here," he patted his stomach and wandered away to settle on a comfy couch. Amused, Lourdes looked up and caught the smiling eyes of equally amused Julie and Luke.

Lourdes and Miguel had slowed the pace of their eating in order not to be the first ones finished. However, now that the dessert was being offered, Miguel hurried along.

"Hey, Mom, I never had the chance to tell Luke about your trip to New York City." Julie requested, "Tell him about your flight, you're the only one who can do it justice,"

"Okay," Katie put down her sandwich and smiled. "The plane trip there was a mess. I'm not normally too nervous travelling, I put my hand on the plane as I'm stepping in from the walkway, and I ask God to send his angels to protect us while we fly. So, I did that.

The flight started out just fine, but then we started hitting awful turbulence. I was soooooo scared! Of course, Tucker wasn't scared. Well, that's what he said, anyway." She tilted her head and raised her eyebrows, letting the listeners know they were to make up their own minds about whether Tucker was frightened or not.

"I think I was scared enough for both of us. And every time we dipped and bumped, I think my face contorted. By the time we landed, I had an awful headache.

I kept thinking if we had died on that plane, I would have had a frozen, frightened expression on my face and you would have buried me like that. You know, friends would walk past my casket and instead of saying how peaceful I looked - they would have commented on how scared-out-of-my-wits I looked."

Katie demonstrated with her arms over her chest, face contorted with fear, eyebrows up, wide-eyed, and mouth open, she stopped talking for a moment and laughed.

Entertained by Katie's self-deprecating story, Lourdes realized most people she knew preferred having a slightly bored look, superior to the people around them – the opposite of this animated, quirky lady. Lourdes couldn't help herself and laughed along with everyone else.

"Anyway, the rest of the trip was fun. I came home EXHAUSTED. All we did was walk, and walk, and walk," Katie said.

Luke laughed. "What? Mr. T wouldn't shell out any money for cabs?"

"Yeah, Tucker did and that was the sad part, because even with that I was still exhausted!" Katie paused with an excited laugh, "Except for the time we were at Times Square and took what we now call...the 'Rickshaw-of-Death.' They're bicycle guys who pull a one-seat wagon thingy, and they charge four dollars per minute.

They get where they're going fast, because they don't care about traffic rules or red lights; they just keep going with you at their mercy."

Just when Katie's voice was becoming excited again, and Luke had the beginnings of a smile in preparation for more of the story, Tucker walked into the room, wiping his hands with a rag, which looked more like it was spreading dirt than taking it off. "I think it's gonna work! I'm ready for this storm!" He walked back into the kitchen after his pronouncement, and they could hear him whistling while he washed his hands.

Tucker sat down, joining them with his dinner. Putting his face over the steam rising from the bowl, he let out a very satisfied, "Ahhhhh." Then looking at his son-in-law said, "Luke, I saw Archie Dallas a few days ago, and he wanted to know when you were going to come back and work for him." Tucker smiled and added, "Of course, I told him that you had moved up to the big time and wouldn't want to come back to such a small potatoes place like Kingsville anytime soon."

"Mr. T, why did you tell him that? That was a great summer job! Someday, I hope to be as good a boss as he was to me."

Maybe it was the teasing tone in their voices, but Lourdes believed this father-in law and his son-in-law got along really well.

"You? A boss? Do you think someday you're going to open your own computer company?" Katie asked.

Luke raised his hand to waive off the idea, "No, no, no. I meant in my department. Someday, well, I assume I'll be promoted. My end-of-the-year evaluation was positive, and they seem to think I have a good future with the company."

"Now those are the kind of words you want to hear from a son-in-law!" Tucker raised his glass of sweet tea in a toast toward Luke, "EMPLOYED!"

For the first time since Lourdes had arrived the group was quiet. Maybe the silence gave Katie the opportunity, but her voice and face both seemed to fall as she said, "Julie, I need to tell you something before we go to church tonight. It's Avy Faye. Her cancer is back."

Julie's response was instant. "What? Oh no! When did you hear that?"

"Just last week. She's as optimistic and as even-keeled as ever, but I wanted to tell you before you saw her at church tonight." Katie despondently looked down into her mostly empty bowl then stood up to return it to the kitchen.

Lourdes could sense a gloomy cloud envelop the table. Katie exited the room with her shoulders slightly drooping. Julie seemed stunned into speechlessness. The others turned introspective. Feeling uneasy, not belonging in this intimate moment, Lourdes looked to Miguel, who gave every sign of reacting the same way as Lourdes felt, and they both sat perfectly still.

Julie broke the somber silence. "Mom, I don't think we're going to church with you tonight. Caleb is asleep, and I think he is probably down for the night. And if I have my way, that's what I want to do, too. Be down for the night."

Lourdes had forgotten there was a baby in the house. She took a fresh appraisal of Julie, who was wearing sweat pants and a polo shirt. Luke wore jeans and a tee-shirt. Lourdes thought they'd look just as at ease dressed up for a dinner party as they did sitting here tonight.

Julie was thin with long, brown hair. She didn't have any baby weight left as there wasn't an unsightly ounce on her body. Luke was tall, blond, and seemed to have found some of the baby-weight that had escaped Julie.

"Lourdes and Miguel," Katie said, her voice raised a bit as she turned her attention to her new guests.

Having been sitting quietly as though eavesdropping on the family chatter, Lourdes, startled at being addressed, jumped a little in her seat.

Noticing the bounce, Katie said, "I'm sorry, dear! I didn't mean to give you a scare. I was just wondering if you would you like to go to the Christmas Eve service with us. It's a small church and the children are going to do a program. The church is right down the street. We'll be there and back within an hour, well before the weather turns bad."

Katie's dad, half-jokingly, barked, "Who's the preacher tonight? If that Reverend that normally fills in over Christmas is there, I'm not going either. He talks too much. He thinks my spirituality is proven by how long I can sit my behind on that pew!" Katie assured him that this truly was a children's program with Christmas carols, a couple of cookies, and a time limit.

"Well, who *is* the preacher now?" Cracker leaned toward Lourdes and Miguel as if telling them a secret. "You never know. Preachers are like football coaches. They stay five or six years and either leave for a better team or they get fired." He laughed at his own wisdom or his opinion of the ridiculousness of some church people.

Nodding his head in agreement with himself, and looking around the table to see who was with him, he added, "Church politics can be a dirty business. Just like the politicians who are ruining this country with all their self-righteous bickering and wild spending."

Lourdes broke into a small grin as she listened to his lively anger.

Katie quickly interrupted him. "Dad, the pastor is still Aaron Anderson, and he is really nice. To be honest, tonight I think Aaron's dad is going to be there and when that happens they tend to let him lead. BUT," she said emphatically, "it won't be any longer, or any different, no matter *who* is leading."

Lourdes didn't exactly know what she and Miguel would do if they stayed home with Julie and Luke. Those two seemed like they would be going to bed, leaving Lourdes and Miguel alone together while it was still early in the evening.

"Sure, I'd like to come," Lourdes piped-up and looked over at Miguel who was also nodding his head. It occurred to Lourdes that she didn't know why she should feel weird about staying here with Miguel, he had been nothing but kind.

"Great! I need to go tidy-up my face and then we'll be off," Katie said, getting up from the table.

The rest of the group went to their own rooms, which were in the guest corridor alongside Lourdes and Miguel's room.

Lourdes and Miguel went to their room together. Although it was sparsely decorated, it had the all-important en suite bathroom, which wasn't any larger than a standard-sized closet. The double bed with an antique dresser sat beside a pale, silvery-blue chair. There were pillows of different sizes and colors strewn across the bed, and a tall reading lamp graced the bedside table. The warm beige wall color paired with the light copper and blue bedding created a tangibly homey and inviting space.

"Nice room," Miguel commented as he looked around.

"I think we're lucky to be here," Lourdes sighed with an air of relief. "Do you want to go to church with them?"

Miguel wobbled his head side-to-side. "Kind of, but not really. I'd rather go to bed. But it seems the right thing to do."

"Me, too. It'll be less than an hour long and it's Christmas-y. I wouldn't mind doing something that felt a little bit like Christmas."

"It's a Tender Tennessee Christmas - just like you wanted." Miguel smiled as he caught Lourdes's eye and tossed his backpack onto the dresser.

Soon after, the group was piling into Tucker's SUV for the three minute drive to King's Community Church.

Leaving the driveway, they turned right onto Jimbo Jack Road, drove a long country block, and turned right onto Deacon where they could see lights inside the three other churches that called Kingsville home.

The parking lots of the First Baptist Church, United Methodist Church and St. Anthony's Catholic Church were all within a few hundred yards of each other, and all four churches (including King's Community) had a smattering of cars.

"How big is Kingsville?" asked Miguel.

"Kingsville, Tennessee. Population one thousand, four hundred and forty-seven fine folks," Tucker replied as he parked the car.

Lourdes knew people who had as many *Facebook* friends as this town had people.

Cracker took his time exiting the SUV. "Hurry up!" Ginny said, laughing. "Come on, do you want me to goose ya?"

King's Community Church was an old, small, white frame building with a weathered cross on top of the steeple.

As they entered the foyer of the sanctuary, a young black boy, probably a first-grader, stood by the door. He wore a dark blue suit with a matching tie. "We're under a Tornado Watch!" he said with all the excitement of someone finding an unexpected Christmas present. "They've had tornadoes five counties away from here! We have an ice storm warning because of an arctic blast coming from the north!" With a much calmer voice, he finished, "Here is your bulletin. Merry Christmas."

"Merry Christmas to you, too!" Katie said as she gave the boy a hug.

Katie whispered to Lourdes, "That's Eli. Best greeter - of any age - from any town – gives a weather report with every bulletin!" Lourdes and Miguel followed Katie toward the front of the church where they all sat on the wooden pews.

A few minutes later, Pastor Aaron Anderson stood at the front of the church welcoming everyone to the Christmas Eve service. He introduced his father, Able Anderson, then motioning to an older woman, Pastor Aaron asked, "Sister Hessie, are you ready?"

Lourdes watched the pianist - whose gray hair barely touched the collar of her simple blue cotton dress - head toward the piano, but before arriving she took a sharp turn toward the left. Quickly, she corrected her direction and sat down on the piano bench.

Katie leaned toward Lourdes and whispered, "She had a hip replacement last year and ever since then - she veers left."

Nodding at Sister Hessie, Pastor Aaron lifted his arms to begin the music. She began to play, *O Come All Ye Faithful,* but the congregation had turned to the song listed in the bulletin, *God Rest Ye Merry Gentlemen.* There was an immediate collision of melody and words.

Cracker leaned toward the elder pastor and loudly said, "We're all singing a different song."

Looking confused, Pastor Able practically yelled in reply, "What do you want me to do about it?"

The congregation adjusted, and they all joined Sister Hessie in singing, *O Come All Ye Faithful.*

As the notes died away, a curly-haired, pre-schooled aged girl in a lacy green Christmas dress walked to the front of the church, saying, "Let us pray. Dear Lord. Please bless the turkeys . . . and the men that will shoot them. Amen." She opened her eyes, smiled a dimply smile and said, "Here comes the manger scene. This is Joseph. He is called the German Shepherd."

Cracker, along with a few others, couldn't contain their stifled snorts and snickers.

Soon, two older elementary-school aged children playing the part of Mary and Joseph walked onto the stage. The girl gingerly carried a baby doll wrapped in a white scarf; the boy, seeming humiliated and downtrodden, shuffled in like he would rather be anywhere but here.

They were joined by six or seven other children with towels wrapped on top of their heads. They were probably all supposed to have white towels, but three of the boy shepherds (who Lourdes guessed were related) had used aquatic themed beach towels. She could see little fish swimming on their turbaned heads - making them look like they were balancing goldfish bowls. They sang, *Away in a Manger,* and sat down.

The pastor's wife, Mary Frances, stood up to pray. She fairly sang her prayer. Lourdes wasn't sure why it felt like a song, but it was the first prayer she'd ever witnessed that made her believe it would be heard.

Lourdes thought, given the chance, she would pray that her wayward, run-away mother would come back for her.

With a touch of despair, Lourdes was reminded of how she was cheated in the genetic lottery, never momma's little girl, never daddy's little darling. She bit her lip as a familiar cloud of disappointment crossed her eyes.

The pastor gave his short Christmas message, which was the cue for one of the little boys with the fishbowl turbans to go back up to the front, reciting, "And the angel said, Glory to God in the highest and on earth peace among men with whom His favor rests."

Pastor Aaron came back to the pulpit and said, "How about we sing hymn #104, *God Rest Ye Merry Gentlemen,* and then enjoy our Christmas cookies back in the Fellowship Hall?"

They all happily sang the familiar carol, filling the church with childlike melody. Of course, only after Sister Hessie had once again veered left on her way to the piano.

The assembled congregation seemed anxious to get back to their respective houses, either due to the impending storm or the kids waiting for the impending visit from Santa.

On their way out the door, Lourdes watched Cracker as he shook a man's hand, patted the fellow's tummy and said, "I see you haven't lost any weight," which he said just as fondly as if he had wished the fellow the most Merry of Christmases.

Ever the cultural mediator, Katie leaned over to Lourdes and said, "I think at a certain age the filter comes off, and you say whatever thoughts are floating around your brain."

The man, who must have been good-natured, just smiled and responded, "Merry Christmas."

In the car, Katie turned to Lourdes and asked if she had enjoyed herself. Lourdes politely replied, "Yes, I did!" The thought occurred to her that she actually had enjoyed the service in spite of having to momentarily relive her family sorrow.

As if it were an after-thought, Katie said to her husband, "Tucker, I invited Avy Faye and the guys to come over if the electricity goes off."

"Well, I invited Polly and Peter for the same reason," Tucker chuckled as he turned the SUV toward their bed & breakfast.

They grinned mischievously at each other.

Lourdes was tired and ready to be lying down. This had been a much more pleasant Christmas Eve than she could have hoped for, and on the whole, leaving her more happy than sad.

The driveway to Safehaven looked even more idyllic this time. The car windows were foggy and there was lightening in the distance, which seemed the perfect metaphor for her stormy future. But for now she would be in a peaceful, safe place.

Tomorrow, Miguel would drive her home, and hopefully she could figure out something to tell her aunt - unsure if she would then even be allowed to stay the night.

She shook her head as if to flick out any thought of babies and her future.

Inside, Lourdes and Miguel wished everyone a good night and went to their room. Each took a steamy shower, crawled into bed fully-clothed, and under the warm, heavy covers fell asleep immediately. All the while the booming thunder and wind-driven rain rudely flapped, seeming intent on cajoling the shingles off the roof.

CHRISTMAS DAY

C hristmas morning began when a queasy Lourdes started stirring. Miguel wished her, "Merry Christmas," in a groggy,
sleepy voice.

Getting up to use the restroom, Lourdes looked out of the
window and saw patches of snow covering the low bushes and
thick brush. Heavy ice hung from the eves, and even in her semi-
nauseated state, she fancifully thought the ice looked like little
mice had hung their finest clothes out on a laundry line, which
was now encased in crystal.

It seemed odd that just last week in Texas her neighbor was
mowing his yard, the scent of freshly cut grass drifting in the air.

They quickly dressed and headed into the great room for
breakfast.

Miguel said, "I guess I should tell them that the bulb in the
bathroom works, but the one in the bedroom is out. Uhhh,
Lourdes, exactly how much per night are we paying to stay here?"

"The magazine said ninety-nine dollars a night, and I have a
five-hundred dollar credit limit on my card. Why? Did they ask
you for a credit card?"

"No. Nobody talked to me about money. But staying here another night is a good idea. I don't think it would be safe to drive out in that ice. Just hope it'll warm up enough so we can leave tomorrow."

Lourdes had kept her credit card, unused, as her future hope, like having a passport with no travel plans. Trapped in a minimum wage job, lacking parents and property, with no clear way to change her life, Lourdes lived with the faint background of an alarm bell constantly ringing – the sound of poverty.

They joined the sound of people chattering and the smell of bacon. Probably wonderful to Miguel, the smell seemed inexplicably overpowering to a squeamish Lourdes. She hadn't had any trouble with morning sickness before and she wasn't sure if that was the problem or if her stomach was unsettled from stress.

Katie, sitting at the end of the long table closest to the kitchen doorway, jumped up as soon as she spotted Lourdes and Miguel. With a cheerful, "Merry Christmas!" she asked, "What would you like for breakfast? We have bacon and eggs, and pancakes with strawberries, and blueberry muffins." She pointed to the credenza sitting by the table. "And here we have coffee, orange juice, milk and apple juice."

Miguel asked if it would be all right if he had just a little bit of everything with some milk. Lourdes gingerly picked up a blueberry muffins and apple juice.

Ginny and Cracker looked up from their bacon and eggs and smiled welcome.

At the long table, baby Caleb had made his appearance. He was chubby, blond, and happy, with big dimples that he often flashed. Throwing Cheerios off of his highchair one by one, he watched them fall to the floor.

"How old is Caleb?" asked Lourdes.

"Fourteen months," Julie said, bending over to pick up the Cheerios. "At home our dog cleans up any stray food. I didn't realize how much work she saves me!"

Miguel, who was picking up one of the Cheerios that had rolled like a bowling ball out of Julie's reach asked, "Where's Mr. Barkley? Checking on the generator?"

Katie stroked the back of Caleb's head and said, "Well, if the generator wasn't working you'd know it by now, because the power is out all over this area. He and Luke have gone over to our friend Polly's house to help get them out of the driveway so they can come over here." Looking out the window, she mumbled, "I hope they get back soon. We need more wood for the fire, and with the weight of the ice and snow on top of the stack, I don't think I can pull it out."

"I can help you with that," Miguel said, standing. "Just point the way."

"Oh my goodness, no! You're a guest here." Katie energetically waved for him to sit back down.

"Really, I don't mind at all. I'll just go grab some wood and come right back in and finish my breakfast."

"Okay, but breakfast first, wood second." Smiling fondly at her guest, Katie poured Miguel more milk.

Lourdes ate her muffin and felt a little bit better, but she hoped the bacon smell would dissipate soon.

Miguel quickly finished his breakfast, got his jacket, and walked with Katie through the red, side door with the lovely stain glass above it that Lourdes so admired. A few minutes later, Miguel returned with an armload of firewood telling Katie, "Really, it wasn't hard to get out. The ice over by the stack was patchy. I put another armload close to the back door underneath the overhang, so hopefully it will start to dry out before you need to use it."

"Thank you!" she gushed. "With all the Christmas preparations... and generator preparations... I guess Tucker forgot about laying some by the back door." Katie started putting the still damp wood into the fireplace, poking it, trying to arouse a better flame.

After they cleared the table of dishes, the group came back into the great room to sit by the now crackling fireplace and the Christmas tree.

"How long have you been here?" Miguel asked Katie, who was sitting cross-legged on the floor with Caleb in her lap.

"Really not that long in the house. We found the land several years ago. When we moved here and started to work on the place, well, the people of Kingsville just immediately accepted us as family!

We lived in a camper while a construction company came with a crane, a crew, and lots of logs on a semi-trailer. They looked like Lincoln Logs! Three days later, we had the exterior of our house. We did most of the interior work." Leaning forward, she added, "And you need to know whenever I say, 'we,' I mean Tucker."

Katie stopped for a laugh at herself. "I did learn one thing, no, a couple of things about myself. I don't like living in a camper, and I don't like moving into a house before it's finished."

Lourdes said, "I don't think anyone would like those things, but the end result here is wonderful! This place is so peaceful!" Her head swiveled, looking around the room, still trying to take it all in, unable to imagine what it must feel like to actually live in such a beautiful environment that breathed tranquility.

"I'd love to say I handled the whole construction process with grace," Katie said, "but honestly, I was a mess. Everything took much longer than we expected and cost more than we planned.

When I get stressed, my eye twitches, and it was twitching so much, I spent half the time with my right hand on my face trying to keep my eyelid still!

Of course, now I think this house is peaceful, and it doesn't hurt that the loudest party in the neighborhood is the guy down the street with his Barbershop Quartet."

Ginny leaned in and said, "And you won't find any bugs in this place. I told them to put a Ziploc bag filled with water above every door and leave it there all winter. They tell me there aren't many bugs in winter, but all I know is that with the Ziploc bags there, well, I haven't seen any!" She nodded her head knowingly.

From behind the Christmas tree a gray cat emerged, batting around a green Christmas ball that had fallen (with feline assistance to be sure) to the floor. Her sister, a brown tabby cat, followed at some distance behind.

Katie glanced at them and said, "Brownie Boo has always been a little more heavy-set than her sister. But we try not to make her feel bad about it. We just tell her that her momma had big hips," Katie laughed. "The brown cat is named Brownie Boo, and the gray cat we call Macey Gray."

Katie explained how she suffered through the death of their dog, Cocoa, and with Julie married and gone, she needed something furry to love. Tucker would have done just fine without any more animals, but he said he loved Katie more than he disliked pets, and drove her to the Memphis animal shelter for her pick of furry friends.

Lourdes wondered if marriage could be filled with respect for the other person's wishes or if it was just Katie and Tucker.

Caleb, who was down from the high chair inspecting the Cheerios on the floor, squealed and started crawling toward the cats. Brownie and Macey immediately left his reach as if they considered him to be on par with a pesky pet visitor.

Julie said, "He isn't walking yet, but he gets where he wants to go so fast that I can hardly keep up with him. Mom tried to baby-proof the house, but it's just impossible to know what he will find to get into." Julie finished up her breakfast with a quick sip of her coffee, now ready for the chase.

Lourdes thought what a lucky baby he was, surrounded by so much love and attention. Closing her eyes for a mere moment, she wondered if she would be able to make her baby feel so loved with no family around.

"Oh! Hey, wait a minute," Katie said, raising her hands and voice, causing everyone to momentarily freeze. "Let me get a picture of Caleb in his Christmas pajamas before he gets them messy.

I need some new pictures for all the frames Tucker gave me for Christmas," she said, running off to grab her camera.

"Where is Cracker?" Ginny asked, sounding annoyed.

"Mom, I haven't seen him since breakfast earlier," Katie called back. Quickly locating her camera, she snapped pictures of Caleb playing. One of Caleb still wearing his Rudolph pajamas seemed destined for the mantel.

"I'd better go find Cracker." Ginny winked at Lourdes and said, "He may be an old codger, but he is *my* old codger, and I have the papers to prove it!"

Excited, Katie said, "There! That's a great picture! Julie, stand still, so I can get one of you and Caleb admiring the Christmas tree."

Julie, now holding Caleb, turned around and faced Katie.

"No, no . . . I mean turn around. It was so cute the way it was. Face the tree, not me." Laughing and waving her hands in a circular motion, Katie added, "I don't want your . . . frontal . . . I want your . . . buttal."

Lourdes laughed and mouthed the word 'buttal' toward Miguel, who was also laughing.

Miguel offered to take a picture of all of them in front of the Christmas tree. However, clicking back on her camera to view her recent snaps, Katie bobbled her head happily and told Miguel, "No, thanks."

Miguel continued, "Mrs. Barkley, I meant to tell you, I think the light bulb is out in our bedroom. The bathroom light works, but the bedroom one is out. If you'll give me a new bulb, I'll change it out for you."

Lourdes had figured out that Miguel was always happy to help.

Katie answered, "Oh, that's sweet. But that's not it. When the generator is on that means only certain things get power: the bathroom lights, the a/c heater, a few things in the kitchen, and maybe most importantly the TV and satellite! That's all the wattage the generator can pull." With eyes sparkling, Katie added, "It's so hard to overcome the love of creature comforts!"

The little group began to disperse, getting ready for the day ahead. Lourdes, alone, stayed in the great room.

She watched as the cats saw the annoying child leave. The gray cat, Macey, jumped onto one of the dining chairs, which scared Brownie, who was walking nearby. Brownie froze, not knowing where the movement came from. Macey, seeing Brownie looking intently frightened, also started looking for the source of danger. Both of the cats crouched, tails bristling.

Ginny, returning to the great room, saw both cats on high alert with their heads rotating from right to left, and also began to look around. "Cats have a sixth sense and can feel things that we humans can't. I'm not superstitious, but sometimes I watch the cats and I think this house was built over an Indian burial ground." With a twinkle in her eye, she continued, "But I don't mention that to Katie or Tucker because they love it here."

Lourdes, knowing the cats only had each other to blame for their panic, and unsure if Mrs. Ginny Philpott was being serious or silly, changed the subject. "Um...Did you find your husband?"

Before Ginny could answer, Tucker opened the front door. With him was a lovely black couple with two small children. Lourdes recognized the little boy as the one who handed out bulletins and weather reports at church.

"Merry Christmas!" said Katie, who had heard the whirl of new guests and was now jogging toward the door. "Hurry up and come inside!"

The man's smile brought as much warmth into the room as the fireplace. Carrying a poinsettia, the woman held out her free arm to hug Katie, while the two children, holding gifts, stood by, quietly waiting for further instructions.

"Avy Faye! How great to see you!" squealed Julie, who had emerged with Caleb, now wearing his Christmas finest. "You two, come here!" she said as she hugged the quiet, well-mannered little boy and girl.

"Lourdes, I want you to meet our good friends, Jesse and Avy Faye Blue and their children, Eli and Angela."

Eli wasn't wearing the suit he had worn at church the evening before, but he was still well-dressed with crisp khaki pants and a blue long-sleeved shirt. His younger sister, who must have been only a year or two different in age, had passed off the gift she was holding to Tucker and was now holding firmly onto her mother's leg. Angela had short hair adorned with a red and green plaid headband that matched her dress.

Lourdes said to the little boy, "I think I saw you last night at the Christmas Eve service."

Eli replied, "I saw you. And I was right about the weather!"

"You sure were!" Miguel said as he entered the room.

"And this is Miguel," said Katie, pointing to him as though she was Vanna White and he was a new prize puzzle.

After a few more, "hello . . . nice to meet you," greetings, the family took off their heavy coats.

"That fire looks wonderful!" Avy said, stretching out her hands for warmth.

"I think there are a few presents underneath the tree with the names of Eli and Angela," sang out Katie.

Eli and Angela looked anxiously toward the tree, but their father said, "I think you'll have to wait until after lunch."

The kids looked up at Katie to gauge her opinion, who said, "Ummmm. You know, I think it might be all right to go ahead and open them."

Katie winked at Jesse. Seeing their father had been over-ruled by the spirit of Christmas cheer, they scampered to the tree where Julie helped them find their gifts.

Tucker said, "We need to go back out and help Polly and Peter get out of their driveway. There are trees and branches down everywhere. I saw Archie while we were out, and he said the power is shut off to all the power lines. So I think I'll take my chainsaw out and buzz a trail." He imitated using his chainsaw going through a tree, looking like a baseball player taking a practice swing. He looked at Jesse and said, "Want to come back out with us?"

The look that Avy cast Jesse clearly said, 'No, please don't,' and Jesse declined.

"I'll go!" Miguel answered quickly.

"Oh my goodness. Seriously! You're a guest here. You really don't have to help!" insisted Katie.

"I really do want to go. I just need a thicker coat. The jacket I brought isn't ready for this kind of weather."

Tucker, thrilled with the prospect of more people using power tools, said he had a coat, gloves and hat for Miguel out in the workshop, where they also grabbed another hacksaw and chainsaw. Looking like winter-worn soldiers marching through the snow, they left the comforts of home to fulfill their mission.

Jesse walked over toward the children who were now sitting by the Christmas tree opening their gifts. It occurred to Lourdes that Jesse looked a lot like Chris Tucker, and like Miguel, he seemed to have a lurking smile just waiting for an opportunity to shine.

"Mr. Philpott, how are you doing?" Jesse extended his hand to Cracker Philpott, who had made his appearance and was now sitting by the Christmas tree.

Cracker answered, "Terrible. My back hurts. I have problems with my feet. I'm going to the foot doctor the end of December."

"I'm sorry to hear that," Jesse said, looking at Cracker's feet sympathetically.

Katie walked over to the children, handed them each a cookie and whispered, "Santa didn't want any more cookies last night so

I saved them for you." Eli and Angela happily took the frosted Christmas tree shaped sugar cookies.

Eli started playing with the *Hot Wheels Motor Speedway* that he had unwrapped while Angela was looking inside her new princess backpack.

The oven alarm started beeping, terrifying Brownie Boo, who was currently running for her life. "When that cat gets scared she goes to her super-secret hiding place, but the thing is, we all know exactly where she goes."

Katie chuckled and pointed to a couch that had some fabric upholstery touching the ground, allowing Brownie Boo to hide safely underneath its folds. "She thinks it's super-secret, so we pretend we don't see her. But her tail usually sticks out about three or four inches." Sure enough, the cowering kitty was easily spotted by her gray and black striped tail.

"Hey, I'm going to get our turkey out of the fridge and finish up our dinner. Avy, Julie, Mom - you're all welcome to help - or not," Katie said with a wave of her hands.

Ginny, Avy Faye, Julie, and the baby Caleb followed Katie into the kitchen.

Jesse and the kids played on the floor around the Christmas tree close to where Lourdes sat.

Only now, with the daylight, did Lourdes spot the scene out the very large picture window. With a catch in her breath she exclaimed, "What a beautiful garden! I bet in the spring time it's awesome!"

The three sections of the U shaped home created a cozy feel to the house. The base of the U was the great room with the long dining table. The left leg was the guest wing, and the right leg of the U was the kitchen and Katie and Tucker's bedroom suite. The outdoor space, encircled by the three sections, was a garden. French doors, close to the long dining table, led into the enchanting space.

Jesse, too, looked out the window, admiring the now-frozen fountain and all the icicles hanging down from the eves and said, "They call it Jim's Garden."

Lourdes asked, "Who is Jim?"

"Oh, he was the base chaplain when Tucker was in Iraq," answered Jesse.

"Tucker is in the military?"

"No, no. He was a civilian contractor, but he had to come home when Katie's dad had a heart attack."

Unexpectedly, Eli said, "My mom has cancer." He continued playing without looking up.

Jesse, who was still peering into the snow and ice-covered garden, looked at his son, smiling weakly.

Lourdes, who didn't know what to say in situations like this, managed a timid, "Yes. I heard something about that."

Eli said, "You can't catch it. It's not like a cough or a sore throat."

Jesse motioned his son to come to him, picked up Eli and lovingly sat him in his lap. With a squeeze he said, "Right, mom has cancer and they have medicine they're going to give her to make her get better. And we are going to pray very, very hard."

Eli didn't respond, but kept his eyes on the new car he was holding. Maybe it was through the stroke of Jesse's hand on Eli's hand, but Lourdes could feel how wordlessly father and son communicated both fear and comfort.

After a moment, Jesse said, "Hey, tell Lourdes about our Christmas. What did you give your mom for Christmas?"

Angela, who hadn't seemed to be paying attention, did not look up from her coloring and answered, "Reading books and puzzle books."

"Oh, that's nice. I bet she loved them," answered Lourdes, happy to be talking about something else.

"Yeah. She said she couldn't wait to start them!" Eli spoke up while scooting off his dad's lap to return to play with his toys on the floor.

Jesse asked, "So what brought you and Miguel here on Christmas?"

"Well, we just got married . . ."

"You're on your honeymoon?" Jesse interjected in a surprised voice.

With a shrug she stammered, "Uhhh, we got married in Las Vegas a couple of days ago – and when I heard the Amy Grant song, *A Tender Tennessee Christmas* – we just decided to come to Tennessee for Christmas on a whim. Then we needed to get out of the bad weather, so here we are."

"Amy Grant? My mom LOVES Amy Grant!" Angela said excitedly.

"Avy does have a neat story about meeting her. You should ask her to tell you what happened. Where are y'all from?" asked Jesse.

"Texas. We're from central Texas and we do sometimes get some ice and snow, but only like every few years, so this is really different for me. It would be awful to try to drive through it."

"Nobody with any sense ever likes driving through it. Here you came for a tender Tennessee Christmas, and instead you found weather from the Polar Express!"

Katie and Avy Faye came back into the great room, a wonderful aroma wafting along – even in Lourdes's estimation.

Instead of remarking on the scent of the upcoming feast, Jesse said, "Katie! You didn't tell me you had some honeymooners staying here!"

"Honeymooners? I didn't know I had honeymooners here! They called and said they needed a place to stay for the night and what with the weather - and the holiday - we thought it was only right for them to be here!"

Angela said, "Mary and Joseph had to stay in a barn because they wouldn't let them in."

"There was no room at the inn, honey. An inn is like a hotel and they didn't have any extra rooms for Mary and Joseph to stay there," explained Jesse.

Katie chimed in, "And we couldn't have Lourdes and Miguel staying in a barn, now could we?"

Angela innocently looked at Lourdes saying, "Did you have a baby last night like Mary?"

"No, no babies last night," answered a sheepish Lourdes. These clearly were religious people who might not take warmly to her situation.

Luckily for Lourdes, the subject changed. Katie, looking a little anxious said, "I hope they can get Polly and Peter out of their house pretty soon. Everything will be ready at one o'clock."

At twelve forty-five, as though they knew exactly what time Christmas dinner would be ready, Lourdes watched as the rescuers swept in with their band of three new faces.

First to be ushered in was a much older woman with deep wrinkles on her face, who had a slight stoop to her walk. Her long braids circled on top of her head in a bun. It was hard to put a finger on her race or heritage, she was simply ancient.

Katie squealed, "Big Momma! Where did you come from?"

"We found her home *alone*, and told her that wouldn't be acceptable, and brought her along," Tucker answered, while taking off his coat and gloves and walking quickly toward the fireplace. All the newcomers were making the same bee line to the warming fire.

In a weathered, whispery voice Big Momma said, "Oh, I was just fine. I heard a knock on my door, and Tucker wouldn't take no for an answer." Lourdes thought her face wore an etched trace of a smile, or maybe it had settled as a joyful shadow over time.

Big Momma didn't seem an appropriate name for her, she was tiny. By her appearance, Lourdes now guessed she must have been full-blooded American Indian.

Katie again did her Vanna White imitation, saying, "Lourdes, this is Bennie Beaver. We all call her Big Momma. Everyone does."

"She may be little in size, but she is big in heart," Jesse said with a squeezing hug. As Jesse stood with his arm around Bennie Beaver, he lovingly looked at her and said, "She loves God. She smokes a cigar at least once a week. And I'll bet she slept barefoot last night - even though it was freezing."

The aged woman smiled and nodded. Her eyes were so dark they seemed almost black in color, which made their contrasting twinkle even more dazzling. "Please just call me Big Momma," she said to Lourdes.

The other new woman in the group said, "Darlin,' my name is Polly, and I couldn't possibly be more pleased to meet you here in this warm house!"

Polly's drawl was as thick as Lourdes had ever heard, sounding like she was from Georgia or the Carolinas. She had silvery-white hair. Lourdes had the assumption she was a great cook and had sampled many of her own tasty treats. If there were a smiling contest between Polly, Miguel and Jesse – it would have been a tough call.

Peter, Polly's husband, had gray hair. He was a big, burly fellow who looked like he had seen hard work in his lifetime, his soft-spoken manner was directly opposite to his tough exterior.

Polly excitedly chimed, "As soon as I heard Tucker's voice, I told Peter that we were *saved*! I've been hearing about this *Craigslist* generator. Now I'm going to have electricity for Christmas y'all!" she said with her most infectious laugh. "I had told Peter that all I wanted for Christmas was for the lights to work!"

Spotting little Angela and Eli playing with their toys by the Christmas tree, Polly bent down and said, "Oh, come over here and give me a hug!" She opened her arms, wrapping up the two children in a big-bosomed hug.

"To get true lights here you have to go to the bathroom. That's the only light fixtures that are connected to the generator." Tucker chuckled.

"That's okay. That's okay. I'm gonna be happy to see them!" Polly was animated in her speaking and hugging. Lourdes was willing to bet she enthusiastically embraced all areas of her life. "I've brought a honey ham with my own special sauce. It can be served at room temperature or you can warm it up a little if you want. Y'all, it is yummy!"

"Dinner is almost ready. We're having turkey and dressing, sweet potato fluff, green bean casserole, and pecan pie." Katie seemed to be saying the menu to the group, but it appeared she was thinking out loud to make sure everything was done.

"And my spiral honey ham that was my Memaw's special recipe," Polly added.

Because of the power outage there were no twinkling Christmas tree lights, but the fireplace and the candles set around the room gave everything a happy glow. The battery-operated Christmas wreath over the mantle still had a happy shimmer. Lourdes thought about her family back in Texas. They might have more warmth and electricity, but their home had never been so charming.

Katie said, "There won't be any fine china today. The dishwasher isn't connected to the generator, so we will be having some very fine, heavy-duty, disposable paper plates. Hope that's okay! Even if the plates are paper we're going to use our regular forks and knives. I really hate eating with plastic forks."

Tucker called them together for a quick prayer. Katie used the poinsettia that Avy Faye brought as a centerpiece for the beautiful table. The meal was served in the kitchen, and the dessert and drinks were set on the credenza by the table. The serving bowls and platters, white pottery with small blue cornflowers, were filled with mounds of food. Even after everyone filled their plates, there was plenty left over for seconds.

The baby, Caleb, had a high chair filled with all his food cut down to finger-food size. Julie had an iPhone that she set in front of him to watch *Baby Einstein* while they ate. "This has saved me so many meals. He is fascinated with it and laughs at the same spots every time he watches it. I don't know what he finds so amusing, but these finger puppets really tickle his fancy!" Caleb, oblivious to the fact that he was usually the center of attention, didn't notice all eyes were smiling at him.

"Well, tell me Miguel and Lourdes, what do you do?" Polly wanted to be the first person asking a question so she could get a few bites in before she started doing most of the talking - as custom dictated that she would.

Miguel looked at Lourdes, who remained silent. Miguel answered, "My family has a mobile restaurant business. We make tamales, tacos, rice and beans. Mom is the best cook in town. Everyone in my family does something different to help out, but I drive the food truck to different business and construction sites."

Lourdes knew Miguel was being modest. That is what he did, but he kept the old truck running along with everything else. It was a good family business. They all made a good living. The now deceased Roy would be missed, terribly missed, but not as a hard-worker. He never added that kind of value to the family.

Polly looked at Lourdes, prompting an answer from her. "I work at a movie theatre. I've been doing that since high school."

Jesse said, "And here they are on their honeymoon looking for a tender Tennessee Christmas!"

Miguel looked quickly at Lourdes, who hadn't had the opportunity to tell him part of their secret had been disclosed. To avoid any further discussion of the sort, Miguel hastily said, "I met Archie Dallas while we were out. He was doing the same thing Mr. Barkley was doing . . . helping people get out of their houses and driveways.

He reminded me of a distinguished judge from a 1950's movie or something."

Luke said, "You know, he kind of does! I never thought about him that way."

"Well, I just saw an old Christmas movie and he looked like one of the characters," Miguel mumbled.

Tucker added, "I don't know what this town would do without Archie Dallas Farms. Or what he would have done without the town after his wife died."

Luke started laughing, "Do you know what he told me his helper said? Mr. Dallas called him last week when he hadn't shown up for work and he - what was his name...Uh . . . Walrus. Anyway, Walrus told Mr. Dallas he couldn't get out of bed because his eyes were bleeding.

Apparently, Walrus had been getting drunk so often lately that his eyes were always bloodshot. Mr. Dallas let him go because he doesn't trust him to drive his truck, or anything else for that matter. He wanted to keep him so Walrus could have a chance to improve his life, but I guess Walrus wasn't going to do that."

Lourdes had seen plenty of bleary-eyed people at work and was never really tempted to drink.

"Luke, what do you do?" asked Miguel.

"I graduated from college a few years ago with a computer engineering degree. I like it. I've always been interested in computer programming, and I work with good people."

Julie chuckled, "After work he stays off of his computer as much as possible! I think because he sits in front of one all day, he doesn't want to look at one in the evening. And that's fine with me! I need help with the baby."

Lourdes could believe that. She had only seen Caleb awake for a few hours, but he seemed to require constant attention. Even if he was just being cute, he seemed to need some help even with just that.

Even though Eli was more the age of a child who would watch a movie like *Aladdin*, he was more interested in the *Baby Einstein* video that Caleb was watching than eating. It must have been the funny part because baby Caleb broke into a wide grin and looked around the table to see if they wanted to share in the humor.

Angela leaned over and put her head on her mom's shoulder, "I know what the lightening was last night."

"You do?" Avy asked, with a responding hug.

"It's God's flashlight."

Eli wasn't interested in even pretending to eat anymore. "Can we go outside and play in the snow?"

"I don't know sweetie, it's really icy cold outside, and I think tomorrow might be a better day to play. What did the weatherman say about tomorrow?" asked Avy.

"No more snow with a slight warm-up," answered Eli.

Turning to Lourdes, Angela added importantly, "Sometimes when we go play in the snow, and we kind of sink down in it, we call it quick snow!"

Lourdes smiled back at the young girl.

Hopping over to a new subject, Avy giggled, "Did you notice Jane's sons with those *Finding Nemo* beach towels on their heads? I just had to laugh. I talked to her after the Christmas Eve service. She said she told the boys to go get the white towels and didn't think to look at them until right before their part in the skit."

Lourdes remembered the shepherds with the fishbowl turbans with a grin.

Caleb's *Baby Einstein* show had stopped and he was now banging on his highchair tray to see how high the food would bounce, saying, "Hi-yee, Hi-yee." Julie quickly put on *Baby Einstein* again.

"What is Jane doing today?" Katie asked.

Avy knew they planned just to stay home so the boys could open their presents and play at home. The whole community knew what weather was headed their way and had made preparations accordingly.

By this time, Polly had finished her seconds of sweet potato fluff and ham and was ready to talk. "It's all so stressful this time of year. So, a friend of mine told me about this Yoga DVD. I went to *Target* and bought one a couple of weeks ago. I tell you it is hard. The lady on the tape said to put your right arm out and your left leg in, well, I felt like I was doing the *Hokey-Pokey*! I couldn't get it right! I did what I thought she said, but I looked nothing like her.

Then the lady did something called the Proud Warrior stand, but I looked more like a Funky Chicken."

After a swallow of sweet tea Polly continued, "For years, I've been getting the vapors. But I've come a long way in conquering my imperfections. Before if someone didn't have a positive comment on my new dress, well, I would have to go home and put an ice pack on my head.

The Yoga tape has helped reduce my stress level, but no one will ever have the honor of being allowed to watch me!"

"The one thing that would help me with my stress level is a good nap," Julie said, while taking the baby out of the highchair. Adding, "Caleb let's go nite, nite."

That was the cue for everyone to scatter. After the table was cleared off, and the leftovers safely sealed in the refrigerator, most of the group gathered in the great room while others went to their room for a nap.

It took a fussing Caleb a moment to settle down. When Julie went to check on him, she said she found three or four of his stuffed animals lying on the floor, picking up one of his new ones she brought it back to the great room. "When he gets mad, he heaves his stuffed animals onto the floor as hard as he can, one by one, until all he has left is the white bear, that's his favorite. He learned pretty quickly not to throw him, or he won't get to snuggle with bear when he wants to sleep."

"That's a crazy looking penguin," Katie said, looking at the blue stuffed-animal with a golden belly that Julie was holding.

"Mom, that's because it's an owl," Julie answered with a giggle.

"What?" Katie laughed. "I kept telling Caleb it was a penguin."

Julie said, "So when Caleb goes to kindergarten, he will be the only kid in class to answer 'What does a penguin say?' with 'Hoot, Hoot, Hoot.'"

The rest of the day was lazy. Lourdes silently watched the interaction between the Barkley's and their friends. Miguel, with all the other adults, watched TV and snacked his way into a stupor with the leftovers. Calling it an early evening, Katie and Tucker invited all the rescued guests to stay in the warmth, but they all decided to brave the cold and make the short drive home anyway.

Lourdes knew she was going to have to brave her long drive home tomorrow. Her constant level of anxiety was palpable, like the hum of a motor that was always running, which no yoga DVD could relieve.

THE PINK HOUSE

Once again, morning started comfortably as Lourdes and Miguel stirred underneath the heavy quilt. Until, that is, Lourdes felt queasy from the smell of bacon that was also, once again, wafting through the air. A quick look out the window and they knew they would probably be spending one more night here. The dainty icicles had no tell-tale drips hinting the temperature had warmed the roads.

They dressed, joining the others in the great room. Hospitably, Katie jumped up and prepared their breakfast plates. They joined the conversation already in progress.

"I don't want to wait until the day before my appointment to drive home. We're going tomorrow, and the ice doesn't scare me," Cracker said while finishing his breakfast - still dressed in his Christmas suspenders.

"Do you think the ice will be gone tomorrow?" Miguel, too, was anxious to get on the road, but the ice did worry him. A few years previously, he had driven on icy roads in Texas and wasn't eager to take on a long distance trek under that condition. Then there was also the money issue. "Well, it doesn't much matter, we need to settle up our credit card bill with you, and tonight is really all we can afford to stay," he finished.

"We all need to get going tomorrow," Cracker said bluntly.

Katie looked at Miguel and said, "Tucker and I are going back with my parents. They live in Little Rock. Julie and Luke need to get back, too. So, we all planned on leaving tomorrow. According to the weather forecast, it should be sunny today, so the ice should be melting. I'm sure they'll be taking care of the Interstate, or it will be closed down - and nobody goes anywhere."

A quick knock on the door announced Avy Faye and the children helping themselves inside. "Hey guys! We're still a bit chilly at home, and we hoped it would be okay if we played over here for a little while. Jesse is out trying to help our next door neighbor."

"Of course you can play over here! I wish you had spent the night! Come over here and let me fix you something to eat," a thrilled Katie jumped up to get some extra plates.

Avy smiled, "Honestly, I wish we had spent the night here, too. It was freezing at home, I don't think any of us slept well."

After breakfast was over, Tucker, Luke, and Miguel once again went out to find neighbors who were in need of help. After hearing how difficult it had been for Avy's family, they especially wanted to check on Big Momma.

Lourdes sat on the floor with Eli, Angela, and Caleb, while Avy, Katie, Julie, and Ginny sat blissfully enjoying their hot coffee. Eli asked, "Will the lights be back on today?"

"We don't know, sweetie. I hope so," Avy Faye answered gently.

Katie said, "Avy, we're all leaving town tomorrow and won't be back until after New Year's. You should stay here. We can leave you the keys to the house, but I can't promise the generator will keep working without someone keeping an eye on it."

"Oh, we'll be just fine." Avy's voice seemed to always have a naturally quiet, soothing tone.

Eli and Angela were burning off some energy by starting to skip around the large room.

Katie said to Lourdes, "I'd imagine that you're anxious to get home."

That's when the most unplanned, honest answer Lourdes ever gave emerged from her lips. "No, not really. I'm pregnant and I haven't told my aunt." Lourdes blurted with a loud sigh. "My mom left a long time ago. I don't even know who my dad is . . . so my aunt took me in . . . even though I'm not sure she wanted to. They won't want my situation." She made air quotes around the word 'situation.' "I'm not sure I'll have a place to stay when I get home."

It was a simple, nutshell pronouncement of her life that *Readers Digest* couldn't have condensed any better.

After a long, awkward silence Katie said, "Well, sweetie, you have Miguel, right?"

Lourdes continued to fix her eyes at the floor. "Miguel isn't the father. Miguel's brother is the father, but he recently died...and Miguel wanted to give the baby their last name. That's all there is to it," she said flatly.

The children, playing with their new Christmas toys, were oblivious to the conversation. Eli, running around the room pretending he was an airplane on a mission, was cautioned about running in the house.

Katie said, "I don't know what to say to help you. But you mustn't lose heart."

Under her breath, Ginny said, "Youth and hormones have always made an unholy alliance," looking at Lourdes with compassion.

Avy moved toward Lourdes to put her arm around Lourdes's shoulder. With a smile and a squeeze Avy said, "You never know how things turn around."

Lourdes tearfully smiled. "It seemed like you're all very religious, and I thought you'd . . ."

Katie interjected, "Well, I know me, and I can promise you that I'm *NOT qualified to be judgmental*," she finished with a wave of her hand as though she were surrendering to the police.

Lourdes wiped her eyes and her nose with her sleeve, which were both beginning to drip and drool a little.

Avy broke the silence which had again settled over the conversation. "Have you seen a doctor yet?"

"No. I don't have any insurance. And, I don't know, it will seem more real when I go."

Avy said, "I used to volunteer at a pre-natal clinic in Memphis, and I'm sure that there must be one in your town. You'd best start getting check-ups and taking vitamins."

Lourdes, now eager to end the conversation, said, "Yeah, I'll check into that when we get home."

Julie piped-up, "I hope we all get to go home tomorrow." She raised her voice a bit to say, "Eli! Hey, Eli, do you know what they're saying about the weather for tomorrow?"

Eli importantly raised his voice in return, "The temperatures are warming, and we will be above freezing today. Tonight, the temperatures will dip down close to freezing, but a warming trend is in place."

"Last year his Christmas gift was a hand-cranked, battery operated NOAA Weather Radio, which he keeps with him in times like this," Avy said, smiling.

"Well, that's some good news!" Julie was anxious to get home. She told Lourdes how they could have brought their dog, but decided that travelling with a toddler was enough and didn't want to add a dog into the mix. Their small black dog with a brown face, named Shirley, had been boarded at the vet's office in a suite decorated with a Christmas theme.

Standing up, Katie gently called to Lourdes, "Come with me for a minute." Lourdes complied and followed Katie through the kitchen. "I'm glad you're here," she said. "I want to show you a picture that's hanging in my bedroom."

They walked into Katie's living space, a large room with high ceilings. A queen-sized bed with thick, cushy, colorful bedding greeted her eyes. In the corner of the room sat a small, velvety pink couch with a matching chair facing a large flat screen TV hung on the wall. She could see there was a doorway that opened into a large bathroom and closet area. The space had an almost tactile feeling about it: warm, cozy and serene.

"Here," Katie said, and pointed to a watercolor picture on the wall close to her bed. "This is what I wanted to show you."

The picture was of a young girl walking peacefully along a watery-blue brook. She was dressed in soft, fanciful clothes, wearing a hat with a long ribbon floating in a breeze. Gentle sunshine and birds in the sky framed the feeling of tranquility.

Katie said, "There was a season when I felt lonely and abandoned by friends and the people I thought loved me. Then one day, I came across this picture. This girl is how I wanted to be. See - if you look at her - she is all alone, but perfectly contented to be that way.

I wanted that for myself, but I didn't have it. I felt like I needed someone to walk alongside of me to feel contented, or, ummm . . ." Katie looked up into the air as if she were searching for the right word, but couldn't find it. Giving up on finding the perfect description, she continued, "Well, I felt like I needed someone else to think I was special. I thought if other people thought I was special that would prove that I was. So, I bought this picture and I would just stare at it, wishing and praying that she was me."

Lourdes was floored. Standing here in Katie's room - which was utterly different than the chaotic clutter Lourdes came from - Katie looked like she had it all. Perfect home, perfect family, perfect friends. There was no way Katie could understand the depth of loneliness she felt.

Katie continued, still unable to take her eyes off of the picture, "A few years later, I started to figure out that God was enough. A relationship with an invisible God was *truly* enough to satisfy my soul."

Looking tenderly at Lourdes, and giving her arm a soft touch, Katie said, "I hope you find that God is enough for you, too."

As they walked back into the great room, Lourdes thought it was nice of Katie to try and cheer her up, but Katie couldn't understand. There was no love from God or anyone else to make everything okay.

Lourdes didn't know if it was out of kindness or contempt, but none of the ladies spoke to her about her pregnancy when she and Katie returned.

Within hours, the guys came back with Big Momma in tow. Slightly exasperated, Tucker said, "We found her at home, COLD, opening a can of pork and beans with her manual can opener!"

"Well, that will never do!" Katie said, echoing Tucker's thoughts. She walked over to her old friend and continued, "Let's see if we can do better than pork and beans."

Big Momma sat in one of the comfy chairs, and said, "I like pork and beans."

"Where is Miguel?" Lourdes asked, noticing that he hadn't come into the house with Tucker and Luke, thinking he must be just a step or two behind.

Big Momma answered, "That man of yours is off with Archie Dallas helping some people on the other side of the highway who are stuck in their houses. He should be along in an hour or two. He's a good man. He makes for good company." Her gentle, raspy voice indicated her affection for her new friend.

Sure enough, about an hour later, Miguel returned with Mr. Dallas, who looked exactly as Lourdes expected; older, wire-framed glasses, not very large, his shirt tucked into his dress slacks. She doubted he had ever worn his shirt hanging out over his slacks a day in his life.

"Were you able to help the Griffins?" Tucker asked, while collecting their coats.

"Oh, yes. Oh, yes," Archie Dallas answered with a chuckle. "Fine help you sent me." Nodding toward Miguel, repeated, "Fine help."

Tucker, also nodding toward Miguel, said, "Fine help he's been to us, too."

Miguel's face flushed, as though unaccustomed to so much positive attention.

Lourdes could see he was inwardly warmed by these nice words from two such honorable men. When Miguel excused himself to go back to their room, Lourdes followed so she could let him know their secret was out. Unconcerned, Miguel shrugged it off.

When they rejoined the others in the great room, the murmuring conversation quieted. Lourdes instantly knew they must have been talking about her. In that moment, she felt sickened that they were gossiping about her behind her back.

Mr. Dallas looked at Miguel, "I've just been told that you two have found yourselves in a predicament. Maybe I can help you. I just had to let my helper go, and I need someone who can take care of various things that come my way. Sometimes I need a driver to take things from the farm into the city. Sometimes I need a mechanic to look after things that break down. Sometimes I need someone to feed the animals...different things every day. Would you be interested in staying and working for me?"

Miguel was shocked as he stammered, "I don't know. I don't know. I really need to be getting back home. My family expects me back . . ."

Tucker shuffled his feet and added, "Well, even if you decide to go back – I was wondering if you and Lourdes could stay an extra few days here. Katie and I have to go with her parents back to Arkansas, and I'd feel a lot better if Big Momma and Avy and her family had a warm place to stay.

I expect that Polly and Peter will be along sometime today, too. If you can stay and make sure the generator is working, and the fireplace going, I'd feel a lot better. We should be back on the thirty-first, so you'd be back home on January first."

Lourdes, wide-eyed, felt as though she was watching her life become a ping-pong ball and had no control over where it would bounce.

"I . . . I . . . I think I'd like to talk to Lourdes and call my parents. Is that okay?" Miguel answered, looking at Lourdes.

"Well, of course it's okay! That's exactly what I'd do!" replied Tucker. "Hey, wait, as further incentive, if you stay, how about we say the nights you were here are a gift from us?" Tucker bowed his head and held up his hand as though presenting an invisible gift.

Dumfounded, Lourdes was unsure of what she had just heard, questioning what it meant to her life, followed Miguel back to their room.

As Lourdes and Miguel were leaving the great room, Katie whispered to Lourdes, "Sometimes if you change your situation - your environment - your location - your friends - it helps you to find out who you really are, and what you want to do. Just a thought."

It was with that thought that Lourdes began to feel even if Miguel didn't want to stay here, maybe she could. Maybe there was some job available in this community she could do, even if it wasn't working for Mr. Dallas.

Miguel's thought process was conflicted. "I feel like I should go home and help my parents. I'm not sure they can deal with Roy dying and me staying away. But everyone here is so nice . . ."

Lourdes added with a squeak, "I know! It's like living on *Sesame Street*!"

Miguel smiled, "Well, I haven't met *Oscar the Grouch* yet, but I think I'd like to help them until the first of the year. Yeah, let's stay and make sure that Big Momma and the others are okay and safe. It's just a week."

Lourdes, startled when Miguel said '*we*' can decide, had an inkling of hope, in a possible continuing ally in Miguel.

She listened in while Miguel called his parents. Without telling them about the baby, he said he needed a little time alone before he resumed regular life. They weren't happy about it, but knowing about the icy weather, they didn't argue.

It was with smiling faces they went back into the great room and told everyone of their decision to stay for the next few days and be the caretakers of Safehaven B&B.

"You don't really know us, so I'm surprised that you trust us this much. But," Miguel paused, "we'll do our best not to disappoint you."

"Well," Tucker answered with a sly smile, "you have lots of eyes watching you."

The following morning was bone-chillingly cold. The power was still out in the surrounding area, and the rural roads might be treacherous. Lourdes and Miguel said goodbye to the bundled-up group of travelers.

Miguel tended to the wood for the fire while Lourdes cleaned-up the breakfast dishes.

Tucker had set a lock and security alarm on their private living quarters. He said it wasn't that he didn't trust them, or any of his guests, but he and Katie had made a promise to treat their area as if were a separate home.

Jesse drove into Memphis for work, leaving Avy and the kids, Polly, Peter, and Big Momma, who would all be staying at Safehaven until their electricity was working.

After the breakfast dishes were put away, Lourdes returned to the great room where there was an argument already in progress.

Eli said, "Nobody can count to infinity!"

Angela haughtily answered, "Oh, yeah? God, Jesus, Holy Spirit."

Eli snorted, "I mean nobody on earth."

Angela retorted, "They're on earth."

Eli yelled back, "I know that!"

Angela, sensing her victory, was filled with pride. "I can count to infinity, plus two."

Infuriated, Eli said, "You cannot! Nobody can!"

Angela placidly replied, "God, Jesus, and the Holy Spirit can."

Eli had just about all of this conversation that a young boy can handle. He searched his vocabulary for just the right word to wound his opponent and end this debate. "You're so . . . So . . . SO . . . BORING!"

Angela laughed. If that was the best he could do, then she had won.

Avy intervened, "Listen. We're going to be together for a few days. I want us to spend quality *time* together not have quality *fights*. Okay?"

Angela looked at Eli and said, "I'm NOT going to be your sister anymore! I'm NOT going to invite you to my birthday! And I'm NOT going to invite you to my wedding!"

"Oh, yeah?" Eli replied, "When you're old, you'll forget you said that! By the time you're in high school, YOU'LL FORGET!"

Avy, not-so-quietly, said, "Hey . . . stop."

The kids took off, running toward their bedroom where there was the sound of a slight skirmish, ranking probably only a 2.1 on the Richter Scale.

Angela ran back crying, "Eli hitted me!"

Avy calmly asked, "Eli. Did you hit your sister?"

Eli earnestly said, "No, Mom. Really, I didn't."

Avy, ever the gentle soul could still give the perfect 'mom look.' She raised her eyebrows and bent her head slightly forward, and asked him again.

"Well, I didn't exactly HIT her. I just sort of took my hand. And made a fist. And sort of pushed her."

Avy closed her eyes and sighed heavily.

Jesse called to say he had arrived from the treacherous drive into work.

"What does he do there?" Lourdes asked Avy when she was off the phone.

Avy told Lourdes about Jesse's job as a personnel manager for *FedEx* at the Memphis International Airport, which was their super hub, making it the largest cargo operation of any airport in the world. He had a good reason to go to work even on bad weather days, so he could save his days off for when she really needed him.

"A few days from now will be one of those times I really need him." Avy showed no emotion as she told Lourdes about going into Memphis to see if her veins were good enough for the chemo or if she would need a port put in for her appointments.

"I constantly worry how this will affect the children," Avy Faye told Lourdes when Eli and Angela couldn't hear.

Lourdes was surprised at this admission. That Avy Faye could speak of her worries out loud seemed courageous. Lourdes didn't want to give voice to things that might make her uncomfortable or her eyes teary. But maybe she wasn't the only one dealing with more than she could handle.

Lunch and dinner came and passed quietly. Miguel kept vigil over the generator and the fireplace. The rest of the group worked together to cook and clean and help entertain the kids. Jesse made it safely back from Memphis, even though he did spin out at one point - luckily not into a ditch or another car.

Avy noticed Lourdes and Miguel hadn't packed enough clothes and had taken it upon herself to call Jane, whose children wore the turbaned fish bowls on their heads, to see if she could help scrounge up some clothes. Her venture successful, Jesse picked the clothes up on his way home from work and surprised a grateful Lourdes and Miguel, who were tired of trying to wash and wear the same things.

As Lourdes rummaged through the new bounty of clothes, she thought how embarrassing it would be to tell Avy Faye if all the clothes were too small.

Her 'Tender Tennessee Christmas' had stretched an extra week, but it didn't change the fact that facing Aunt Connie might be only a few days away. Thinking about it made her stomachache worse.

December twenty-ninth was Avy's appointment to see about her port. The power was still out in Kingsville, but it was back on in most of Memphis. The improving roads meant Avy could keep the appointment in the morning, and since they still didn't want to get Eli and Angela out, Jesse asked Polly and Big Momma if it would be okay to leave the kids with them while he drove Avy to Memphis.

Miguel had gotten a call from Mr. Dallas and had gone to lend him a hand. Lourdes was having a bout of nausea and didn't know if she needed to eat something, lie down, or go to the bathroom and be rid of it all. She opted for trying to lie back into the squishy couch.

"Are you all right, darlin'?" Polly noticed the greenish tone to Lourdes's face. "Can I get you anything?"

"Oh, you know how it is. I think I'm okay, but maybe some crackers would help."

"I'll be right back!" Within a moment, Polly came back with some Sprite and crackers.

Angela surveyed Lourdes, "Are you sick?"

"Actually, I'm going to have a baby. And sometimes that makes you feel funny, and right now I don't feel good."

"Are you going to throw up?" Angela asked curiously.

"Sometimes I feel that way, but then some crackers help." Lourdes was munching crackers, and sipping her Sprite, and was starting to feel a little better.

Angela didn't say anything else about it and went about her business of playing as usual. Half an hour later, Angela called out to Polly, "Miss Polly, I think I'm going to throw up!"

Polly yelled back, "Darlin', go to the bathroom - I'll be right there."

Angela replied, "I think I need to eat some candy to make me feel better."

Lourdes smiled at how smartly Angela had figured out a new system for getting snacks, but just as smart was Polly who figured out Angela's plan.

Later that afternoon, Avy and Jesse came home with good news about the port. Her veins were good enough, and the chemo would be starting January fourth.

Katie and Tucker had called to say they would be coming home New Year's Eve, and that Julie's family had made it home safely. Everything was going fine at Safehaven B&B with rumors buzzing that Kingsville was next to have power restored.

After supper, Avy asked Lourdes if she had given any more thought about going to the pre-natal clinic.

"No, not really. Miguel and I haven't really talked about staying or going. And, well, I've been wondering . . . even if he decides to go home . . . well . . . I was wondering if you knew of any place around here that I could work – and then maybe I could stay."

For Lourdes, saying a comment like that was an act of uncommon bravery. She knew too well the look of rejection that might appear on Avy's face.

Miguel happened to be rounding the corner into the kitchen where the two women were talking and overheard them. "I think I'll stay," he said. "Errr . . . I think WE should stay. Mr. Dallas asked me again today about working for him. He told me he has a rent house that we could live in."

"Oh, right! The pink house!" Avy said as she bobbed her head up and down excitedly.

Miguel shrugged. "I don't know exactly what color it is."

"Mr. Dallas owns a small, pink house not far from here. It's been empty for a while. It's right next to an abandoned store - in beautiful downtown Kingsville!" Avy ended with an enthusiastic smile.

"Stay," Lourdes whispered, almost tearfully. Never had a word sounded so wonderful, she felt a burst of hope she had never known before. She knew this only postponed her inevitable struggle, but gladly grabbed this reprieve.

She and Miguel didn't talk about it. Miguel called his parents and told them that he would be staying for a little while longer, but didn't explain everything. Lourdes called Aunt Connie to say that she was staying in Tennessee and asked for some of her clothes.

Aunt Connie, without any questions, agreed to send the clothes.

That evening, Lourdes and Miguel went to bed tired and ready for sleep. Miguel told her a story about a rooster that had frozen in a tree during the height of the ice storm. Several days ago, he found it lying on the ground, but the guys told him not to worry about it because it was too ornery to die. Today he found the mean old rooster alive, thawed out, terrorizing anything he could. With a chuckle, Miguel turned over to sleep.

In the middle of the night, Lourdes began to dream, quite vividly, that two men were walking across her front yard while she was home alone. One of the men wore a tank top and had shaving cream all over his face, the other wore blue jeans and a tee shirt. Wanting to scare them off, Lourdes started to yell, "Hey! I see you!" Or maybe, she thought, it would be scarier to bark like a dog. She decided to bark like a dog.

Woken up by a strange sound, she realized that she must have actually started barking, or making some other-worldly noise because Miguel popped out of bed, wildly looking around, unsure of what was happening.

"What? What's wrong?" asked Lourdes.

"I'm not sure. Did you hear that noise?" mumbled Miguel.

"Was it kind of like a dog barking?" asked a self-conscious Lourdes.

"No . . . well, maybe it was. I don't know what it was."

"I was having a dream about bad guys in my yard, and I wanted to scare them off by barking like a dog. I think it was me you heard."

Miguel groaned.

Not knowing if her nightmare noise had startled any of the other people in the house, Lourdes – embarrassed to the point of shame – pulled the covers up to her chin and kept her eyes open in an effort not to go back to sleep. Still, she went back to sleep, quietly, for the rest of the night.

Finally, it was New Year's Eve. Katie and Tucker would be home in a few hours. The rumors the electricity would be back on by lunch in Kingsville proved true. The grateful families who had stayed through the cold all returned home. Lourdes and Miguel took Big Momma back home.

After dropping off Big Momma, making sure all her heating and appliances in working order, Lourdes and Miguel took their first peek at the pink house.

The pink house was located on Market Street, which meant it was three minutes from Safehaven and three minutes from Big Momma. The house was a small, square frame house with fading pink paint and peeling white trim. The dirt and pebble driveway led to a frame garage, which Miguel had been told not to use since it was structurally unsound.

They parked in the driveway and walked down a small, over-grown path to the front door. A large, thick oak tree solidly stood in the front yard. The front door stuck, causing Miguel to give it a hard shove. The electricity had never been turned off, so they were able to turn on most of the lights as they walked around.

The front door opened into a small living room. Lourdes commented, "It's plenty big for a couch and TV!"

Immediately to the left was the dining room with a connecting kitchen. A door to the outside was located beside the refrigerator. She could hear the hum of the refrigerator as she strolled by, admiring her good fortune.

A hallway opened from the living room, leading to the two bedrooms and one bathroom. Everything was old, small, and in need of a good cleaning.

Lourdes thought the place was as beautiful.

Riding back to Safehaven, Lourdes asked, "Where are we going to buy the furniture, the plates, the pans, and things that we need to live there?"

"Well, it might be kind of rough for a while. But Mr. Dallas doesn't need any kind of deposit, he said he'd pay me every Friday, so this Friday we can go buy a bed and paper plates."

Lourdes cheerfully said, "I guess it will be easier to clean that way."

"Or," Miguel added, "you said you have a five hundred dollar credit card limit so if you want to, we can charge our beds and move in tomorrow. But we'll have to do without a lot for a while."

"That's okay," Lourdes breathed. "This is more than I could have asked for." She looked happily at Miguel. "Let's put the beds on my credit card. Tomorrow is perfect." She nodded her head as if agreeing with herself and added, "Maybe they have a thrift store in Memphis. You can get some pretty good things there at really good prices."

Katie and Tucker arrived home safe and sound later that afternoon. "The roads were miserable when we left, a lot of black ice. We were worried for ourselves and for Julie and Luke. Then about fifty miles out of Memphis the roads were perfect!"

"How was Cracker's doctor's appointment?" Lourdes asked Katie.

"Fine. He doesn't like going. He calls it, "being in the clutches of doctors," and said he will never go to a hospital again. I think he means it, too.

My dad complains a lot. He just isn't who he used to be. I feel sorry for him though, he isn't in good health with no real prospect of improvement. He's cranky and sharp-tongued." Katie frowned, adding, "It's just tough to be in his position - tough on everyone... especially my mom."

Tucker came into the room after checking on his prize generator which had helped so many people. "Great job, Miguel! Everything looks great!"

Lourdes joyfully pronounced, "Hey, guess what? Mr. Dallas offered Miguel that job, and Miguel decided to accept it. We're going to stay in Kingsville for a little while!"

Katie responded with a clap of her hands.

"Great! That's just great!" Tucker said, seeming genuinely happy. "You'll be a welcome addition to our community."

Miguel told them all about the pink house, and that they'd be moving out as soon as they could buy a bed.

Katie said, "It's funny, we didn't know you a week ago, but you don't feel like strangers, and we felt so much better about leaving town with you here taking care of our friends."

Even though it was New Year's Eve, no soul at Safehaven stayed up to clink glasses and ring in the New Year. The way the previous year ended was far too fatiguing for such merriment.

Lourdes knew back in Texas each member of her family would be eating twelve grapes at midnight and making a wish for the New Year. She hoped that missing that tradition wouldn't bring an ill-fate for the coming year as she drifted off to sleep.

DRIVING MISS AVY

The next morning, Katie asked Miguel and Lourdes if they would like to go to church with them, explaining how King's Community Church always had a New Year's Day service followed by lunch - consisting of the traditional black eyed peas, cabbage, cornbread, and ham hocks.

After agreeing to go, Lourdes asked Katie, "Did you happen to pick up any grapes on the way home?"

"No, but I can pick some up the next time I go to town if you like."

"Well, it's our tradition that we eat grapes at midnight on New Year's Eve, and I didn't do that last night. I just sort of . . . well . . . I don't want to jinx anything."

Katie opened the refrigerator, smacking her lips a few times while she pondered the situation. "Here, this grape jelly claims to have a pound of grapes in every jar. I think if you drink some grape juice, and eat a piece of toast with grape jelly on it, well, that might just do the trick!"

After a quick breakfast, which for Lourdes was a grape-fest, they all jumped into Tucker's SUV and took the short drive to King's Community Church.

When they came to the intersection of Market Street, Lourdes knew if they were to turn left, they would be one long country block away from her soon-to-be new home at 1009 Market Street.

For this particular holiday, not every church in town was having a service. Only King's Community was welcoming in the New Year with a luncheon. There were quite a few cars in the parking lot, probably more than on Christmas Eve. Lourdes wondered if members of the other churches planned to party here today, too.

They made their way to the front door where Eli stood with a bulletin.

"How is the weather?" Miguel asked the world's best usher.

Quite professionally, Eli answered, "We should have a week of warmer weather, but after that there is a chance that the freezing cold will return. We'll have a better computer model later as the week goes by."

Judging by the enticing aroma from the fellowship hall, the congregation had successfully prepared their traditional luncheon.

Katie left them so she could mingle with her friends. Lourdes and Miguel sat a few pews back from the front and studied the bulletin, partly to keep from having to talk to other people and partly not to have any awkward silence with each other.

When Katie sat down to join them, she said she had asked a few folks if they had anything to donate for a housewarming for Lourdes and Miguel, managing to find a few furniture pieces and other whatnots she thought would help them get settled.

Before they could thank her, Pastor Aaron Anderson walked to the front of the church, while his wife, Mary Frances, sat down to play the piano. They sang unfamiliar songs to Lourdes and Miguel, so all they could do was sort of move their mouths as not to appear clueless in the world of Christian music.

Pastor Aaron stood to speak. He was a middle-aged, slightly balding, sturdy man. He seemed sturdy, not only in his build, but there was something about him that gave you the feeling that you could lean on him if needed. Mary Frances was thin, with salt and pepper hair, pretty and well-dressed. Before Pastor Aaron became 'Pastor Aaron' he had served in the military, and he still carried that air of focused determination.

He spoke about the nostalgic feelings of Christmas only to have, within a one-week time period, a change of perspective to the future and hope for the New Year. Pastor Aaron was of the opinion that God had good things in store.

Afterwards, they all filed into the Fellowship Hall. Long tables were used for serving, leaving few places to sit and eat. There were some small, hard-plastic tables for the children, but the adults would have to juggle their plates and iced tea as best they could. Some of the more elderly people found chairs along the wall. Just like each person seemed to have their preordained spot on the church pew - now they all seemed to have a preordained place to stand.

Having filled his plate, Archie Dallas found his way to Miguel. "Are you two moving into the pink house tomorrow?"

Miguel had to swallow fast to answer. "We were hoping to start cleaning this afternoon. Tomorrow, we'd like to go buy a bed and move in."

"Lordy, yes. Good idea. So how about you start working on January third? I have a few things already planned for that day. Sound all right to you?" he said with his typical chuckle.

"Yes, sir. I'm ready to get started!" Miguel seemed genuinely glad.

Lourdes smiled, knowing how much Miguel liked working alongside Mr. Dallas.

Katie brought over a few friends to meet Lourdes.

Jane was the first introduction. There was something fun about her manner that made Lourdes want to smile when Jane spoke. "Katie said you're going to be moving here, and you might need a few things to get started. I can bring some things over tomorrow or the next day." While Jane was speaking, her three-year-old son, Samuel, walked up, crying. "What happened?" she asked, hands on her hips.

Samuel pointed at his six-year-old brother, Steven, saying, "He did it!"

Jane leaned over and whispered with a grin, "I guess it's not always as important WHAT happened as it is WHO did it."

The six-year-old boy sulked over carrying a plastic golf club that seemed to have been the source of the problem.

Jane said, "What should you say to Samuel?

With a frown he said, "I forgive you."

"No, you tell him you're sorry," Jane said, holding a straight face.

Eli, who was ready to go home, walked over to the group and said, "I'm bored."

Katie asked, "Sweetie, what does 'bored' mean?"

Thoughtfully, Eli replied, "That's when everything you can think of to do sounds stupid."

Everyone nodded their head in agreement.

"Sounds about right," answered Jane.

Polly, who had just been told Lourdes and Miguel were staying in Kingsville, strolled over to hug Lourdes and said, "I heard Miguel is going to stay and work for Archie! I think that's just ducky!

You young people must need a few things to set-up housekeeping. Believe me, I must have ten of everything, and I'd be tickled to give you some of my things. At my age, you think more about downsizing than collecting. Neither my Charlotte nor Savannah seems to want any of my stuff.

Charlotte buys too many things as it is. She'll go on a buying binge and hides shoe box, after shoe box, after shoe box in her trunk, so her husband won't find them."

While listening to Polly's generous offer, Lourdes's attention was drawn to a little boy's naked, cheeky bottom scuttling toward

Jane. His pants were at his ankles as though he had his feet coupled in a chain gang.

Jane asked him, "What *are* you doing with your pants?"

Three-year-old Samuel answered, "Waiting for you to pull them up."

Jane quickly obliged. Samuel added, "And, uh, I am only tattling a little. Well, you see, Sarah is chewing with her mouth open."

Lourdes felt charmed by this family and hoped if her little baby misbehaved, she would find the humor - not the annoyance.

After a little tidying, the fellowship hall emptied with some folks going home to watch football and some going home for the first nap of the New Year.

Foregoing a nap, Lourdes and Miguel went to the pink house to start cleaning. Lourdes couldn't be around any chemical smells because of her pregnancy, but she could still sweep.

Miguel brought over some light bulbs to change out the ones that were burned out making any dark or gloomy spaces disappear with the fresh light. Miguel cleaned the only bathroom and asked Lourdes, "What all do you think we'll need to stay here tomorrow night?"

"A bed for sure. Some groceries and toilet paper, towels, pillows and blankets, hey, that sounds like a good camp-out," she said with a smile.

Then a thought occurred to Lourdes with such a thunder, she loudly said, "Wait! There are two bedrooms. Which one do you want?" The luxury of two bedrooms meant they didn't have to share.

Miguel thought about it for a second and asked, "Did you say you had a five-hundred dollar credit card limit?"

Lourdes nodded yes.

He said, "Let's see how much a full size mattress costs versus two twins. And then see how much all the other things cost. If we have enough money, then we can buy two beds – and if we don't – then we'll only buy one. I don't want to be in debt for stuff that we'll only use a little while...we're not staying that long."

Lourdes had shared a room for as long as she could remember. Never had there been the luxury of having her own room or her own things, but Miguel was right and if she had to sleep fully clothed for the next part of her life - then so be it.

"Katie said some of her friends have extra things they are going to give us. Maybe we can wait and see what they bring before we buy a lot. I don't want any debt because of mattresses either. We'll just buy what we can afford," she agreed, matter-of-factly.

Miguel locked up the much cleaner pink house for the night, while Lourdes took one last look knowing that tomorrow she would be living there.

The next morning, Tucker offered to drive his truck into Memphis where they could pick up a bed. Lourdes tried to figure out the logistics and said, "It's my credit card that we're going to use, so I guess I need to go and sign for it. Can the three of us go?"

"If you don't mind a tight squeeze, we can manage. It's a pleasant drive," Tucker answered.

"Okay. But the roads are okay now, right?" asked Lourdes.

Tucker nodded, "Oh sure. Everything's back to normal."

"Also," Lourdes asked while running through her to-do list in her mind, "I need some groceries. Where do you normally shop?"

"If you have a lot to buy, we'll go to the Memphis *Target*, but we tend to buy our groceries right here in Kingsville at the Mercantile on Main Street."

The shoppers found a discount bedding company and bought the cheapest queen-size bed. With the mattress, box springs, and frame, it still cost three-hundred dollars plus tax. There would only be one bed for the pink house.

Lourdes thought how grateful she was that Katie and Tucker hadn't charged them for the nights they stayed at Safehaven. If she had paid for staying there, they would be sleeping on the floor.

After they got back to Kingsville, Lourdes was dropped off at the Mercantile, which was just down the street and around the corner from the pink house. Inside the building, the floor sloped to one side, a bit like Sister Hessie when she veered left.

There was an old-fashioned, wooden pickle jar in the middle of the building. There was a counter for refrigerated items that had meats, milk, butter, a few types of juices, and yogurts and cheese. There were shelves of canned foods and bread. Another section had paper goods and cleaning products. The only worker was a very large, much older man, dressed in denim bib-overalls and boots. He didn't return the smile when Lourdes walked in and smiled at him.

"Can I help you?" he mumbled.

"I just need to pick up a few basic things. Do you take credit cards?" Lourdes asked respectfully, even though he was the first person she had met in town who wasn't welcoming.

"Yes. Cash or credit. No checks. Been burned too many times," he answered suspiciously.

"Okay, thanks." She picked out the things that would make a few basic meals. Two boxes of macaroni and cheese, milk, bread, butter - anything she could use to make do for a few days.

"We're moving into the pink house," she told him while he was sacking up her groceries, thinking that might start a pleasant conversation.

"Umph," he grunted.

"My . . . ummm . . . husband . . . is going to work for Archie Dallas Farms." Lourdes had the idea that maybe he would warm up to her with the mention of Archie Dallas.

"Once he set up a farmer's market right across the street from me and took all my produce business." The man didn't look up at Lourdes when he spoke.

"Oh," was all Lourdes could say.

"I hear that pink house gets really drafty. You're going to be cold living there this time of year. Just you think about that when you get sick," he practically growled.

Lourdes left the Mercantile. Walking back to her house she thought how she must have just met *Oscar the Grouch.*

Mumbling to herself, Lourdes said, "People pay big money to live in the city center and walk to shops." She finished with a laugh, "And here I am doing just that, in the city center of Kingsville, Tennessee!"

Even though it was a short walk, Lourdes thought it would have been better for Miguel to have picked her up since she had three bags to carry. Strangely, Tucker and Miguel weren't at the pink house, but the door was unlocked.

It was empty, even maybe a little scary, but when she saw the refrigerator freshly cleaned and ready to be filled - it made her smile.

She hadn't quite finished putting away her groceries when Katie knocked on the door with her arms full of things for the house.

She brought a handmade quilt from Big Momma, which was the most beautiful quilt Lourdes had ever seen. The colors were soft and it was thick and warm. There were some sheets from Jane. Polly sent cups and dishes. Strangers were donating a couch and chair, which Tucker would bring over later. There were TV trays, a CD player, clock radio, someone's unwanted new kitchen utensils – still halfway wrapped in Christmas paper, and kitchen towels – some used, some new.

"You've moved in at the best possible time!" Katie said, a little breathless from carrying in the various boxes and bags from her car. "People were either getting replacements for some of these things or their houses just seemed so full they knew they could spare an item or two."

Feeling like Christmas had just come and Katie's car was Santa's sleigh, Lourdes bubbled, "This is so amazing! And whatever we don't get, I can go buy from the thrift store after Miguel gets paid!"

There was a rumbling engine pulling into the driveway. When the two women looked outside, they saw Tucker in his truck and Miguel, who was driving a loud, chugging truck with

Archie Dallas Farms written in faded letters across the driver's side door. The two men hopped out of their respective trucks and started to take off the straps holding the bed, box springs and frame.

Outside, Lourdes slowly read aloud, "Archie...Dallas...Farms," as she ran her fingers over the blurry, faded letters on the red 1967 Ford Ranger. "I guess driving this truck is a part of your job?"

"Yep," Tucker answered for Miguel as they hoisted the mattress and began carrying it into the pink house. "We saw Archie a few minutes ago, and he wanted Miguel to go ahead and pick up the truck so he could drive it first thing in the morning."

Lourdes, feeling giddy, said, "I figured that out for myself. Because, well, if it smells like a duck!"

Miguel smiled - and as was becoming normal for him - did not correct her.

Tucker and Miguel picked up the lightweight box springs, and not wanting the pregnant girl to grab anything, asked Lourdes to step aside. When she moved, Lourdes accidentally stepped on Miguel's foot. "Don't worry," Miguel said, "No toes were injured in the stepping on of this foot."

"The man that works at the Mercantile grocery store said this house is really drafty. I know all the appliances work, but does the heater work?" Lourdes asked, hoping that Tucker might know something about the house.

"The fact of the matter is that this house doesn't have air or heat. The next hard freeze you can stay with us. I don't think it'll be too bad for the next little while, but you will be chilly. The man at the Mercantile is Clayton Hobbs, and he was, unfortunately, right about you being cold," Tucker answered.

Katie walked outside, and overhearing the last bit of conversation said, "I think I have an electric blanket at home. I'll go home and look for it and if I find it today, I'll bring it back over to you." Unsure of where she last saw it, Katie looked upward as though she might be able to peer into her own brain to find the last memory of the blanket.

With the continued cleaning and unpacking, the rest of the day went quickly. Katie must have visualized the last known location of the blanket because she soon brought it over - along with some leftovers from dinner.

Lourdes warmed up the black-eyed peas and ham, all of which were prepared on a skillet given by a stranger. They sat on the floor and ate their first meal in the pink house.

That night, they were so fatigued they drifted off to sleep easily. Lourdes began to dream. She dreamed the baby was a subway sandwich and when she took the lettuce off, she couldn't remember which side of the sandwich was the head, knowing she couldn't put it back together again was sure everyone would be mad at her. Starting to wake up from the dream, she thought she heard the noise of a burglar breaking in.

Bolting upright, she shouted, "I've got a gun! I'm calling the police!"

Shocked into the realm of wakefulness, Miguel jumped up, sleepily shouting, "Who has a gun? Who has a gun?"

Lourdes shushed him, whispering, "I think someone is in the house, and I'm trying to scare them off."

Shaking off the shock of the moment, Miguel walked through the house fussing, "Lourdes, there isn't anyone here. What do you think you heard?"

"Well, I was dreaming the baby was a subway sandwich and..."

That was sufficient. He cut her off, saying, "Oh. Okay." That's all he said as he lay down.

The following morning brought a feeling of excitement as Miguel was looking forward to his first day of work. Lourdes cooked him scrambled eggs and toast, and since this was her kitchen, she didn't have to endure the smell of bacon. Luckily, there had been an old toaster in the bag from Katie's sleigh.

The pink house came equipped with a very old washer and dryer. Mr. Dallas had sent a new hose for the washer as a replacement, so the old, dried-out rubber on the current hose wouldn't rupture and flood the place. Lourdes wanted to wash the hand-me-down clothes and the sheets and towels. The first load of wash went fine. She moved the clothes from the washer to the dryer and started a second load in the washing machine.

After fifteen minutes, a buzzer began to sound. It sounded like the clothes in the washing machine were off balance. Thinking she had put too many towels into the wash, she thought maybe she should take some out, but no matter what she did, the buzzer did not stop. No amount of distributing the weight changed the increasingly annoying buzzer.

Feeling frazzled, she called Miguel, who didn't answer his phone. Noticing this was a Kenmore product she called *Sears*. The person who answered the phone told her to unplug the washing machine, and they would send someone out to diagnose the problem. Not having any money for repairmen, Lourdes didn't set an appointment - unsure if Mr. Dallas would approve the charges.

She hung up the phone and unplugged the washing machine. The buzzing continued, even after it was unplugged. By this time Lourdes was in tears. The unbearable, constant noise was something like water torture.

Calling *Sears* again, the person on the phone assured her that unplugging the machine should have disabled any buzzer. Lourdes wailed into the phone, "Clearly, it is not disabled!"

"Ma'am, we can get someone over there tomorrow. Other than that, I don't have any other suggestions."

Tears on her cheeks, Lourdes plopped onto the bed. After what felt like an hour, Miguel called her back. He could hear the buzzing in the background and promised to be right home.

Ten minutes later, Lourdes heard the blessed rumbling of the old truck. Miguel looked at the unplugged washing machine.

Then looking at the dryer, he unplugged it. The buzzer stopped immediately. "Dryers are pretty easy to fix. I'll look at it when I get home tonight."

Embarrassed to the core, she thanked Miguel for coming.

Lourdes called the seemingly unhelpful person at *Sears,* and with no explanation but with a bit of attitude said, "Never mind coming. We fixed it ourselves!"

Soon after her cell phone rang, she felt glad to see "Katie Barkley" pop-up on the caller ID. "Avy needs a little help babysitting Angela. I was wondering if you could help her out?"

Happy to do something in return for these kind people, Lourdes said yes without hesitation. "But I don't know where she lives," she replied.

Katie answered, "Oh, she is going to drop them over here. I have to leave for a few minutes, but I'll be right back. We really only need you for that little bit."

"I'm on my way!" Lourdes hung up, took the keys to Miguel's Honda, and sent him a quick text.

At Safehaven, the Christmas tree and the decorations were all gone. Even though some of the twinkle had been removed from the great room, it still shimmered. There was no fire in the fireplace, but the golden sunlight streaming from the windows seemed idyllic. Always a happy, peaceful place, it occurred to Lourdes that the walls of this home had absorbed the personality of the people who lived here.

As soon as Lourdes opened the door to Safehaven, she saw Angela holding up a half-colored page in her new *Disney Princess* coloring book. "Look what I did!" Angela said.

"Well, why don't we color together? You pick the page and I'll color the page across from it."

With a promise to be right back, Katie left them sprawled on the floor, coloring.

Pretty quickly, Angela had colored all she was going to, and climbing onto the couch, started jumping.

"Does your mom let you do that?" asked a wary Lourdes.

Angela got a serious look on her face, leaned her head forward toward Lourdes, and whispered, "She's not here." Angela's face had a hint of surprise that Lourdes could be so naïve as to not realize the obvious fact that rules are fluid depending on who's watching.

"Well, why don't we *not* jump." Lourdes wanted to laugh, but thought that might lessen her credibility.

They were just deciding which game to play when Katie returned and Lourdes went home to the pink house.

Miguel came home from work around 6 o'clock. Lourdes asked, "Is this going to be your normal time to get off? Do you work like 8am through 6pm?"

"I think it is going to vary depending on what he needs done for that day."

"Oh," Lourdes replied. "How do you feel about the job? Do you like it?"

"Well, today, we were setting up an inventory listing on his computer. I just used the same format I used for my parents at the restaurant. He seemed to like it and was really grateful. I don't think he has had many people working for him before with much computer experience," Miguel answered, washing his hands.

Lourdes listened to the details of his day while they ate their dinner. She had baked some potatoes and stuffed them with ham, cheese and butter. "Well, I wasn't wondering so much about the forms you filled out as I was wondering how you felt while you were filling them out."

"How I felt about filling out forms?" he asked quizzically.

"Yeah. Like, how did you *feel* about your day?" She said the word 'feel' quite demonstratively.

With a shrug and a blank expression, he answered, "I guess I felt okay about it."

Lourdes cleared her throat. "I called my aunt today, and I told her that we were going to stay here. I didn't tell her about the baby. She seemed really surprised and kept asking me if I was okay. I told her that I liked it here, just wanted to try a new place for a while. She asked me did I quit my job at the cinema, and I told her that I'd call and quit. Then she asked me if I wanted to be taken off their phone plan."

Lourdes looked down at her plate. It wasn't until that moment she realized how hurtful it was that Aunt Connie's main comment about her moving out was about the phone plan.

Miguel must have realized Lourdes was upset. "Mail her your cell phone back. My phone is on my family's plan. I guess I need to see if I can keep mine or not. Don't worry, we'll figure out something. People lived a long time before cell phones and they seemed to manage. Maybe we can get a land line. I'll ask Mr. Dallas tomorrow.

For now, I'll give you mine and if you need me, call Mr. Dallas – he will know how to find me."

Miguel didn't seem to fluster easily, and Lourdes liked that about him. Still, there was no doubt that she needed to find a job. Some extra cash would help pay for food and phones.

Lourdes was practiced in the art of worry and worst-case-scenario. Worry fit right into a world filled with twenty-four hour news programs instilling fear of terrorism, sickness, and getting e-coli from touching raw potatoes.

"Okay," she said, "I'll walk this phone over to the post office tomorrow. Anyway, I've been thinking about finding a job here. I need to do something that'll make extra money. Tomorrow, I'll ask Katie if she knows of anything."

By this time, Miguel had handed her his cell phone and was looking through his wallet for the phone number to Archie Dallas Farms. Lourdes took the phone and typed in the number Miguel handed her.

With a frown Miguel said, "Wait, hand it back. I need to call my parents and tell them the whole story about why we're here and ask about the cell phone."

He left the kitchen and walked outside where the weather was uncomfortably chilly. Forty minutes later he walked back inside. "They're not happy. After I told them about Roy's baby . . . well . . . they want us to move back there so you can live with them, and they'll take care of the baby after it's born."

"They want to raise my baby?" Lourdes furrowed her brow so much it resembled the pleats on top of a drapery.

"I think they would take care of you AND the baby. I'm not sure that's the future you have in mind. Don't get me wrong, they're good people, but I think they do want the baby. Maybe that's what you'll want later, too. That's up to you. I just told them, for now, we're staying here. They said I can keep the phone."

Miguel took a long breath and mumbled, "The car is paid for, the insurance costs eighty-five dollars a month, the phone is free, rent and utilities are part of my salary. That means I need to earn enough for food, gas, and insurance."

"Miguel, I'll find some work, too. At least until the baby comes and I figure out what to do. Right now . . . I just want to thank you for being here with me. I don't know what would have happened if it wasn't for you." Lourdes's voice cracked a little.

Embarrassed, Miguel looked down at the floor and offered no response.

Lourdes's soon-to-be-returned cell phone rang. Katie's name popped up again. "Hi," answered a still emotional Lourdes.

"Hey, we need a favor, but I think it will help you out, too," Katie said.

"Sure. Whatever you need," Lourdes responded, feeling more in control of her feelings.

"Avy needs to go into Memphis tomorrow for her first chemo appointment. I'm taking Eli to school and then I'll watch

Angela here. Jesse *was* going to take Avy, but now he can't do it because of his work schedule . . . and we were thinking . . . maybe you could ride with her, and she could show you the pre-natal clinic so you could start your check-ups. If she's feeling sick or really tired after the treatment, she'll need someone to drive her home."

Lourdes wouldn't have minded driving Avy Faye, but the added part of having to go to the doctor herself did not sound good. She knew she would eventually need to go, but TOMORROW? Deciding she could take Avy, but then invent some excuse not to go to the clinic appeased her apprehension.

After a slight hesitation Lourdes answered, "Ummm. Yeah. I can do that."

Sounding grateful, Katie asked Lourdes to be at Safehaven at nine in the morning.

"All right, see you then." Lourdes ended the call and told Miguel, "I'm going with Avy to her chemo appointment tomorrow, but she wants to show me the pre-natal clinic so I can have my first check-up . . . I'm NOT going to do that part!"

"Well, I think you should probably go," Miguel said matter-of-factly as he got up to fix the dryer buzzer.

The pink house was cold and drafty just like the old man at the Mercantile had promised. The electric blanket was their salvation. Luckily for the residents of the pink house, there were no crazy dreams or shouts of guns that night.

Miguel's work day would start at eight in the morning unless Mr. Dallas requested otherwise. The semi-flexible schedule would be based on whatever the to-do list dictated. Since the farm was only a few miles away, the commute time was less than ten minutes.

Arriving on time to Safehaven, Lourdes saw Avy Faye's car already there. Hugging Lourdes, Avy said, "Thanks for doing this! You're a life-safer."

"Well, your chariot awaits!" Lourdes said with a smile. She asked a nervous looking Avy Faye, "Are we going very far from here?"

"It's close to forty minutes each way. I thought we could drop by the clinic first and get you set-up for an appointment."

Lourdes had a glimmer of hope that she wouldn't feign a lame excuse about not seeing someone today. Making an appointment wouldn't be so bad, maybe in a couple of weeks she would feel ready.

Walking outside, Avy said, "If you're comfortable driving my minivan it wouldn't cost you any gas. I can drive us there, but on the way home it's possible, well, probable, I won't be feeling good." Avy endured this before and knew the wicked nausea.

Lourdes looked sympathetically at Avy and nodded. "I'll drive on the way there, too, so I can get used to your car, if that's okay," Lourdes said as her cell phone rang. The name 'Atufftt' came up. "Atufftt?" she mumbled, and with a questioning voice answered, "Hello?"

"Hey," said Miguel's voice. "I was wondering if you'd left yet. And I wanted to tell you Mr. Dallas thinks we'll finish around four o'clock today."

"Okay, thanks and we're just about to go. Hey, when you called just now the name 'Atufftt' came up on the caller I.D. What is that?" Lourdes asked.

"I don't know. What did you type in for the phone number?"

"I thought I put in A D Farms. Maybe that became Atufftt? Well, I'll see you tonight."

Since the clinic was a little closer than the hospital, they went there first. It was a nice trip and, as always, Avy Faye's gentle ways were easy to be around. Avy wasn't overly chatty and seemed content to sit quietly at times. Her minivan was easy to drive, and the traffic in Memphis wasn't too dreadful.

"I was expecting the traffic to be worse," Lourdes said, a little relieved.

They pulled into the old, crumbling concrete parking lot of the *Good Samaritan Pre-Natal Clinic*, which was a free-standing, yellowing brick building. Their sign read: For low income women. Free to the neediest and most vulnerable women and babies.

Lourdes felt small and sad knowing that described her perfectly. She couldn't deny those were the facts of her life, but she didn't like seeing it on a sign for the world to see.

Avy must have been sensing her worry. "Let's go in. I've volunteered here before. Everybody is really nice."

Inside the small waiting room was one pregnant woman who had two other small children with her. The girl behind the reception desk saw Avy Faye and immediately jumped up to give her a hug. "Hi!" she squealed, "What are you doing here?"

"I've brought you a sweet friend of mine who needs to be here." Avy pointed at Lourdes, who smiled a pathetic smile. "She's going to need an appointment for her first check-up."

"Hum. Let's see," said the kind-faced girl. Lourdes noticed her name tag said 'Peggy.'

"Actually, if you can wait around for a little while we can do it today. I think the bad weather we've had sort of threw everyone off. We shut down like everyone else did, and I don't think people know we're open again."

"No. No. I have to drive Avy to an appointment, so I can't do it today," Lourdes said hastily.

"You can take me and drop me off then come back after me. It's not far," Avy said to Lourdes, then turning to Peggy added, "She can be back within half-an-hour if that works."

Inwardly fuming, Lourdes thought it presumptuous and rude of Avy to force her to go in for an appointment. Although it was hard to stay mad at her when they pulled up to the hospital, and Lourdes realized how awful this day must be for this exceptionally quiet and sweet woman, who would soon have toxic chemicals pumped into her body in the hopes of killing cancer cells.

Avy Faye gave her the directions of "Turn here, or drop me off there and when you pick me up – I'll be down the hallway to the left."

Lourdes begrudgingly plucked up the courage and went to her appointment.

Back at the pre-natal clinic, Lourdes walked through the door to be warmly greeted again by Peggy. It seemed any friend of Avy's was a friend of hers. "Let's get you started filling out the medical forms and then we can get you back for a check-up."

The forms were standard forms and Lourdes got at least one smile from herself when she thought about asking Miguel how had he *felt* about filling out forms. She didn't *feel* good about it at all.

A few minutes later, she was standing on a scale and her weight and blood pressure were recorded. Peggy said, "We have rotating, volunteer doctors that come regularly. Sometimes, you'll see a mid-wife, but if there is anything that the mid-wife doesn't feel comfortable with, then she'll send you to a doctor. They're all very nice and only want you to have a good pregnancy and deliver a healthy baby."

The doctor today was Dr. Marsha Mason, who said, "Lie back and let's see how things are going for you." After a very uncomfortable exam – Lourdes had never had anyone in her "area" before – the doctor looked over the forms and said, "From what you've told me, your due date will be August sixteenth."

Knowing there was an actual due date for the baby, Lourdes felt equal measures of excitement and anxiety.

Dr. Mason put the clipboard in her lap and with a professional calm asked, "What kind of relationship do you have with the father?"

For whatever reason, Lourdes didn't seem to mind telling this complete stranger the circumstances of her life. "Well, he died. I just married his brother so the last name would be right for the baby, I mean, we're not together. It's a long story, but we're going to stay in Kingsville for a while - maybe until the baby is born - and then I don't know what I'll do. Probably go home to Texas."

"Do you know the sexual history of the father?"

Stammering, Lourdes answered, "What? Well, no, I guess not." The question seemed inappropriate and embarrassing.

"I generally suggest being tested for STD's. Even if you think you know someone's history, you don't always, and I want to make sure of things like that for the health of both you and the baby. Will you consent to testing?" Dr. Mason's expression wasn't judgmental, just matter-of-fact.

Flabbergasted, Lourdes gave a weak nod. An STD? Roy had seemed so romantic. A popular boy was paying attention to her. It was true they had never been on a real date, but when he picked her up from work he was always saying nice things to her.

Wanting to change the subject, Lourdes said, "Um. A couple of weeks ago, I swallowed a ring . . . and I kind of choked." She waved her hands over her throat and continuing, said, "Then we got a metal detector to see if it was stuck in my stomach. But the detector acted like it was going down." She waved her hands over her stomach, and noticing the doctors' expression, decided not to explain further. "And I'm wondering what I need to do about it."

"Well, I imagine you passed it already, but if you have any pains in your stomach, or side, or if you start running a fever we would want to know about that."

Dr. Mason kindly didn't press Lourdes on the matter, although gauging her expression, the doctor was very curious about the metal detector comment.

After leaving bits of blood and urine for testing and getting a list of vitamins she needed to start taking, Lourdes left. Still reeling from the thought of an STD, she went to pick up Avy Faye.

Lourdes drove back to the hospital and found the double doors to the wing that administered the chemo. The doors had a yellow bio-hazard/radiation sign, along with other signs, clearly indicating that pregnant women should not enter.

The hallway was lined with benches. Some of them were filled but most were empty. Lourdes picked a bench and waited for Avy Faye.

Sitting within ear-shot of Lourdes was an older woman with someone who might have been her daughter. The older woman said, "That one looks like he's about to die." She spoke loudly enough that the gentleman passing by could easily have heard her. "His skin color is positively green."

The woman sitting with her didn't respond or even look like she had heard the comment, although Lourdes thought she looked a bit stricken with embarrassment. The older woman seemed oblivious that anyone else could hear her.

A middle-aged woman came walking down the long hallway, accompanied by a nurse. "This is where you'll be coming," the nurse said gently, but straightforwardly. The woman looking frightened, dazed, and wide-eyed, continued through the double doors with the nurse to where Avy Faye was getting her chemo treatment.

Not long afterwards, Avy Faye appeared. "Hi! Did you have to wait very long?"

"No. It didn't seem so long," replied Lourdes.

"I like to go get a little something from the cafeteria before I get in the car to go home. They have really good lime Jell-O. Do you mind if we go? I'd be happy to treat you to something to eat." Avy Faye seemed in good spirits.

The hospital cafeteria was small. Even though it wasn't lunch time, there was still a smattering of people around the tables. Avy Faye got her lime Jell-O, and Lourdes got a Sprite. When they sat down Avy asked, "How was your check-up?"

Lourdes wasn't sure what to say, although so far honesty hadn't been met with an unkind word. "They're testing me for STD's. I don't even know what to think," she answered while she stared into her bubbly Sprite as though it was interesting. "I haven't been with any other person than Roy. I was worried enough about having a baby, and now I have something else to worry about, something horrible."

Avy put her hand on top of Lourdes's. "I'm sure it's just a precaution. Which doctor did you see?"

"Dr. Mason," Lourdes answered flatly as she looked up.

"Oh, she is really nice and very thorough. Don't you feel better that the first visit is behind you and they're making sure that you're healthy?"

Lourdes smiled pitifully.

The ride home was uneventful as Avy, thankfully, wasn't sick to her stomach.

That night Lourdes made spaghetti and garlic bread for supper. She could barely contain herself as they sat down to eat. "Miguel, they tested me for an STD at the doctor's office today. Did Roy have an STD?"

"I don't think he's had anything for a while," he answered not making eye contact.

"NOTHING FOR A WHILE?" Lourdes turned pale. Shock wasn't even the right word. Romantic? There was nothing romantic about the aftermath of being with the popular Roy Rico. How was this even right? How many TV episodes and movies had she seen where people slept together, and they woke up the next day either in love or with no consequences at all? Certainly THEY didn't get pregnant or get an STD. This was not fair. This was not the way it was supposed to be.

"Lourdes, what did you think was going to happen between you and Roy? Actually, you were lucky. I loved my brother, but he wasn't perfect where girls were concerned." Then adding hastily and forcefully, "But I couldn't have asked for a better brother!"

Miguel looked squarely at Lourdes. He had always protected his brother in life and that wasn't going to change now. "You were a lot different than most of the girls he went with. I knew this baby was his. Normally, he was possessive and kind of controlling. He tended to make sure his girlfriends . . . did things his way."

Roy had never been violent with Lourdes. She wondered how far she would have gone, and what kind of behavior she would have accepted from him, in order to have a boyfriend. Her cousin had a boyfriend that twisted her arm when he was mad, and she always made excuses for him, saying she kind of liked that he wanted her all to himself. Lourdes wondered if she would have been like that, willing to endure physical pain to escape the emotional pain of feeling like you weren't being picked for a team.

Neither of them seemed to want to continue this conversation, so the rest of their dinner was eaten in silence.

After eating, Miguel said, "Good spaghetti. I liked the bread. Thanks for cooking." Miguel took his plate and set it in the kitchen sink.

Lourdes felt planted to her chair. Shaky from shock, she remained silent.

From the kitchen Miguel said, "Mr. Dallas sent a couple of electric room-heaters home with me tonight. He said he was worried about us getting too cold last night. I'll go get them out of the truck."

Wearily, Lourdes cleaned up the dishes and joined Miguel in the living room where he sat one of the heaters. Determined not to think about Roy and STD's, she resolved not to discuss it with Miguel again.

Still not having a television, they sat beside a CD player that had been loaned to them along with the *Harry Potter* book series on CD.

"One of Katie's friends loaned it to us," Lourdes said. "Her kids have all the *Harry Potter* series on CD and she said we could borrow them. Have you read the books?"

"No. I don't read very much."

"Have you seen the movies?"

"No, but I'll try it," Miguel answered.

Lourdes had read the books and seen the movies. She loved *Harry Potter,* and it hadn't occurred to her that there was someone who hadn't entered into that magical world. Excitedly, she said, "You're going to love it! After we finish this book, I'll see if we can borrow the next one."

"That'll be good. If we have enough money left after paying for all the other things, we can see about buying a TV of our own."

Lourdes looked seriously at Miguel before saying, "I'm going to find a job. I'm gonna help. I'll talk to Katie tomorrow and see what she thinks."

They went to bed in the drafty pink house, the room heater helping remove the biting chill. In the morning, they moved it into the bathroom where the warmth was indescribably wonderful.

Miguel seemed happy to go to work. The job and his new boss agreed with him. He worked with his hands, he was outside most of the time, he tinkered with machinery, when he was inside he did computer and spreadsheet work, and he helped people - all these things were his strengths.

After Miguel left for work, Lourdes went to talk to Katie, who was babysitting Angela at Safehaven. Curious about Lourdes, she quickly asked, "How was your appointment?"

Pent up tears and fears spilled out, Lourdes blurted, "They're testing me for an STD! I thought it was all so romantic and wonderful to have Roy in my life. Now I think it was ugly and gross!"

Katie softly spoke in reply, "What does romantic really mean?" With a slight smile she said, "Last year, we were babysitting Caleb while Julie and Luke took a few days for themselves. The baby got sick. Tucker slept on the floor beside the crib, just in case the baby woke up and needed something.

I had never been so charmed by him as I was that moment. When you're thinking about boys and dating, you don't wonder what kind of a father or grandfather they might be, but as years go by those moments are immeasurably romantic."

Putting her arms around Lourdes, Katie finished, "Let's see the results of those tests and go from there. Until then, I suggest that we don't borrow trouble."

Lourdes didn't answer, but flattened her lips into a frown and bobbled her head in a meaningless nod, while Katie gave her a small rub on the back.

Angela, happily coloring, was oblivious to any conversation. Lourdes, feeling a little less burdened, perched on the floor beside the sweet girl. "What are you coloring?" she asked.

"It's the story of Jonah and how he got eaten by a really big fish," answered Angela.

Lourdes asked, "How did that happen?"

Angela didn't look up, but answered, "He didn't trust God."

Lourdes asked, "I wonder why he didn't trust God?"

Angela continued coloring and answered, "I don't know. I guess when people get old, they just do that."

Katie said with a smiling chuckle, "Sad - but true."

After a moment, Lourdes cleared her throat and looking down at her hands, said, "Katie, I need to find a job, and I was wondering if you knew anybody in town that was hiring."

"Well, there isn't much going on in Kingsville. You might have better luck in Memphis. What kind of work do you want to do?"

"It doesn't matter. Anything I could do while pregnant, I guess, and something short-term, since I'm not sure when Miguel wants to quit Mr. Dallas and I'll have to move."

Tucker walked into the room, Katie took the opportunity to ask him if he knew of any jobs for Lourdes. Before he could say anything, Lourdes asked, "Actually, Tucker what do you do? I mean I know you run this bed and breakfast, but you always seem to be coming and going."

"A little bit of this and a little bit of that." Tucker's vague answer came with a smile.

Lourdes didn't want to pry.

Then Tucker offered, "After everything that happened to us, we decided to use our savings and build Safehaven. We've mostly finished the inside, but the property still needs a lot of work. You can't see much behind us because the brush is too thick and needs clearing. Folks around town seem to have designated me the town handyman, and I stay busy doing a little bit of this and a little bit of that." He smiled, "The extra money helps."

"Tucker can build or fix just about anything." Katie looked fondly and proudly at her husband.

Tucker asked, "Katie, can you come help me in the kitchen for a minute?" The pair disappeared into the kitchen while Lourdes stayed with Angela.

Katie and Tucker reappeared with a cookie and a glass of milk for Angela, which they sat on the table to make spills more manageable. Lourdes had gotten up from the floor and found a comfy spot in a welcoming chair.

Tucker said, "Avy Faye had a rough night last night from the chemo. She's at home today. I think with her last go-round with cancer she made her appointments on Friday so that she would have the weekend to recover and Jesse would be home with the kids. His schedule is different now that he got that promotion, and he has a rotating-day-off schedule." He sighed, "Scheduling will be harder this time."

Looking at Lourdes, Katie said, "We're all so worried about her, but she wants to keep volunteering part-time at the elementary school. She said she wants Eli to see her doing normal things - so he can know everything will be all right.

Polly can't really watch the kids. Once when Eli was little, and she was babysitting, he fell and bumped his head. It wasn't a bad bump, but Polly was so shaken *she* needed the ice pack and Tylenol more than Eli. So . . ." Katie took another breath, "Tucker was just telling me that several people around town want to collect money to get some help for Avy Faye.

He thinks we could all pitch in together and pay one hundred dollars a week for the next several months. The hours and the job would be whatever Avy needs, maybe a little housework, taking care of the kids or driving her to Memphis. It would just all depend. Tucker is thinking maybe the Lord sent you here to help her. What do you think?"

With a choked whisper Lourdes answered, "You hardly know me and after all the things you do know about me, I feel surprised you'd even ask me."

Katie's expression softened. "Tucker and I have had our fair share of tough times and life experiences. And we think we're a pretty good judge of character. AND, not to seem distrusting, when you babysit it will likely be here, so people will be in and out, kind of like when we locked our part of the house when we were out of town - trust with limits. Are you interested?"

"Oh my goodness! Yes!! When do you want me to start?" she answered amazed.

"Let's make this a week-by-week proposition. Tucker will need to make sure all the funds are collected. You know people say they want to help, then when they open their wallet, well, you know."

Tucker chimed in saying, "No. I know who has said they'd help, and I'm sure the money will be there."

Katie said, "Well then, how about now? We have guests coming this weekend, and if you could take care of Angela I could get about my business!"

Still in shock, Lourdes started her new job by coloring the opposite page of Angela's *Jonah and the Whale* coloring book.

She knew she was only playing-house. Even though this was the first time good-fortune had come her way, she knew it would end. But determined to have some measure of peace in her life, she pushed down the thoughts of how this would all end some day, and decided that at least this day, she would try not to let worry creep around the corner.

That evening over dinner, Lourdes told Miguel that pretty soon she would have money to help pay the bills, boasting her first purchase would be a new TV. He smiled and said, "That's great! I'd like to finish the *Harry Potter* books though."

The temperatures were still chilly, but the forty degree weather felt blissful after the cold nights in the pink house. Lourdes was hopeful the warming trend would continue.

Miguel left for work at eight in the morning, and Lourdes was at Katie's house by eight-fifteen when Avy dropped off Angela.

Avy gushed at how happy and blessed she felt that so many kind people had donated their money to provide help during this season of life.

When Lourdes saw Avy she asked, "How can I help you with your housework?"

Avy, in her natural peaceful tone said, "Would you mind if I brought some laundry over?"

"Sure!" Lourdes said. "If you want, you can bring the dirty clothes in the morning, and I'll take them home to wash and fold at night, and then bring them back here the next day."

Avy hinted how much she appreciated being able to go home alone - preferring privacy when she felt so sick.

After Avy left, Lourdes asked Katie about getting the next *Harry Potter* book.

That night, Harry Potter crept into her ever growing-wilder dreams. In a forlorn mansion, Harry was hiding. Lourdes had the job of finding him some ham to eat, because he liked ham. Walking into a dark hallway, she found herself in an unknown space where Harry would meet her to get the ham. At the same time, a bunch of bad guys came, forcing her to duck into a side room. Trying to use a wand to stop them, she frantically wondered when Harry would come and help.

"Did he come help?" Miguel asked Lourdes in the morning after she told him about the dream. "I don't know. I woke up before it was over," she answered with a laugh.

Miguel was beginning to look forward to the dream stories from the night before - so long as they didn't involve him being sharply awakened with shouts of guns and robbers.

As the end of January approached, Lourdes and Miguel decided that while they lived in Kingsville, they should keep visiting King's Community Church. As they walked in the front door on a frigid, windy Sunday morning, they were met by Eli with the weekly bulletin. "An Alberta Clipper may be headed our way next week. Do you know the difference between an Alberta Clipper and an arctic blast?"

Lourdes and Miguel caught each other's' eyes, stifled smiles and shook their heads.

"An Alberta Clipper comes from the region of Alberta in Canada, but an arctic blast just comes from the north," Eli explained.

With fresh new knowledge of weather systems, they took their seat. Sister Hessie veered left, she found her way to the piano and began playing some worshipful songs that neither Lourdes nor Miguel knew. The variety of voices in the congregation didn't always meld melodically - but there was something lovely about the singing.

Pastor Aaron spoke about the goodness of God. "It was a revelation to me," he said, "when I realized that the Lord is *MY* shepherd, and He calls Himself a *'good'* shepherd.

When the Bible uses the word *good* it means beneficial. He sees our need and promises to provide. It changed my life when I realized that the good shepherd was *MY* good shepherd and would look after *ME*."

This was a different view of God than Lourdes was used to hearing. She was under the impression that God was always kind of hacked-off.

The next week, Eli's weather forecast seemed to be coming true. It was thirty-nine degrees with another ice storm coming.

Katie and Tucker had the generator ready and invited the same Christmas group back, just in case the electricity went out.

By morning, the bad weather had indeed slid into Kingsville. Most, but not all, of the power in Kingsville was out. Polly and Peter, Avy, Jesse and the kids, Lourdes and Miguel, and Big Momma stayed for two nights to escape the bitter cold.

Eli said the best part of the bad weather was that school was cancelled so his mom would be staying home to play with them.

The day started with Tucker's unhelpful computer, which wasn't working quite as fast as he thought it ought. He and Peter had spent the better part of two hours fiddling with the bewildering machine. "I wish Luke was here," Tucker said. "What's the good of having a computer whiz for a son-in-law if he can't come right over and fix things?"

The unfixable computer issues seemed to be taking its toll on Peter, too, who could be heard muttering grumbling words like 'blasted' and 'smack-n-frack.'"

Thinking he could help with the computer, Lourdes looked for Miguel. She found him having issues of his own.

Hearing some huffing and puffing, and some mild cussing coming from their bathroom, Lourdes knocked on the door to investigate - although the cussing would have only generated a PG rating. Miguel opened the door and pointed to a teeny bald spot on the left side of his head. "Don't ask," he fumed. "Can you come here and fix it?"

Ignoring the 'don't ask' part of the conversation, Lourdes asked, "What happened?"

"My cousin normally cuts my hair," Miguel explained while holding the still buzzing razor, "so I borrowed *this* from Tucker." He held the razor higher as if for show-and-tell. "Can you fix it?"

A few minutes later the bald spot was less noticeable, although his hair was much shorter than normal.

Pleased with the outcome, Miguel returned the shaver to Tucker and proceeded to help the guys with their computer woes.

Warmer weather, along with everyone's electricity, returned within a day, and Safehaven returned to being a working bed and breakfast. Since January eighth, the birth of Elvis Presley, they had stayed quite busy as their reputation on *Tripadvisor* continued to bring travelers.

Crockett Elementary was back open for young minds - sending Eli back to school. Lourdes could be found at Safehaven taking care of Angela.

Bored with what Lourdes had planned for the day, Angela said, "I wanna follow Katie around." They found Katie straightening the same room where Miguel and Lourdes had stayed when they arrived on Christmas Eve.

"Like some help?" Lourdes asked Katie, who was changing sheets.

Looking at Angela, Katie answered, "You look like an excellent pillow-fluffer!"

Standing in the room, the thought struck Lourdes how much her life had changed in such an abbreviated space of time. She asked, "Katie, why exactly did you decide to open a bed and breakfast?"

"Well...that's a long story, but I'll give you the short version. Tucker and I had several cleaning businesses. One day, while we were gone on vacation, one of our employees was injured at work. I'm sure she was hurt, but she was back at work a day or two later and seemed fine.

That is until some lawyers convinced her she wasn't fine. Two years later, she and her lawyers had taken everything we owned - including our house."

"They took your house?" Lourdes's jaw dropped.

"Yup. So, Tucker went to Iraq as a contractor and earned enough money for us to build this house. I lived with my parents . . . and then Julie for a while . . . and a few various friends so we could save every penny. Luckily, his pay was great and we were set again.

He would have stayed longer, but my dad had a heart attack, and they weren't sure he would survive. Tucker took the next plane home. The next thing I knew, Tucker was walking down the hallway of the hospital with Iraqi dirt falling off his boots.

After Tucker got home, I fell apart, so he said he'd finish up his eighteen months and come back to stay."

Lourdes, indignant, said, "I can't believe someone would sue you and take all your stuff! You're the nicest people I've ever met! Actually, I think you're the nicest people in the known world!" After a quick breath, Lourdes continued, "Weren't you furious?"

Katie smiled with a sigh, "I won't say we didn't have our moments, but we trusted God would provide a way for us.

We found this land, bought it, and lived in a borrowed trailer while we built this place. It was a simple existence and a physically hard time for us." With a wink she whispered, "Still, it was kind of better than living with my parents."

Katie stopped her cleaning, looked at Lourdes and said, "It was all quite humbling. Not humiliating, but very humbling. But we wouldn't have this wonderful life we have now if we hadn't endured those terrible times. God works all things for our good."

The sound of Angela softly singing filled the pause in the conversation. "Come on Angela!" Katie said as she took Angela's hand and continued to the next room.

Lourdes, who had been thinking about the story she just heard said, "I don't know, seems like a mean way for God to get you here."

"I guess listening to my life flat-out like that, it does seem harsh. But living through it . . . I can tell you - for sure - I felt God's faithfulness. Truthfully, we're in a better situation now than before our trials started."

Lourdes's cell phone rang, it was the pre-natal clinic. After a very brief conversation, she put the phone back into her pocket.

Through teary eyes, she looked at Katie and said, "I didn't catch anything from Roy. I'm okay."

Katie hugged a shaky Lourdes and said, "Glad you decided not to borrow trouble since there wasn't any."

Bashfully, Lourdes hugged her back.

That night, Lourdes told Miguel her good health news. She also told him the story of Katie and Tucker and why they built Safehaven.

Miguel finished his dinner, surprised at how unfazed Katie and Tucker seemed by their past financial troubles. "Hey, Lourdes," he called from the kitchen where he was putting his plate into the sink, "Today, Mr. Dallas had me go over to help Sister Hessie at her *RV and Collectables Park*. She wants you go to over there tomorrow and pick out something from her store as a thank-you. And do you know who Sister Hessie's husband is?"

"No," Lourdes answered. "She's been at church by herself as far as I could tell. I assumed she wasn't married or a widow or something."

"It's Clayton Hobbs. The man who runs the Mercantile grocery store!"

"You mean *Oscar the Grouch?*" Lourdes exclaimed, laughing.

"Yeah!"

Lourdes said, "Wow. Sister Hessie seems so nice, not someone who'd be married to a grouch like him! It's funny," Lourdes continued, "I can't imagine being married to *Oscar the Grouch*. And I would have never thought that Katie and Tucker ever had a rough life."

Joining Miguel in the kitchen, Lourdes said, "I guess you never know the pain behind someone's perfectly put-together church clothes."

Looking at him while he silently helped clean the kitchen, she was struck by how much kindness she had known from Miguel. He was helping her in ways that her own family wouldn't have done. Maybe it was true he wasn't helping HER, but the baby who belonged to his beloved brother, but still, it was life-changing help. A warm smile crossed Lourdes's lips.

The next few weeks flew by with a sense of normalcy. Miguel went to work while Lourdes did whatever she could to help Avy by babysitting, doing laundry, or driving Avy to her Memphis chemo appointments.

It was Valentine's Day. Miguel came home for dinner a little later than usual.

As soon as Miguel came in the door, he handed Lourdes a small, pink, stuffed dog with red and purple hearts scattered over its' cheerful body.

"Happy Valentine's Day," he said with a slight bow.

Surprised, Lourdes accepted the gift from Miguel as their eyes smiled at each other.

"You've been such a trooper, and you do your best to help everybody. Just wanted to show you that I appreciate you." Miguel said the last sentence with a shrug as though what he really wanted to say was that he was glad Lourdes wasn't a whiny diva.

"I went to a grocery store for Mr. Dallas. The place looked like it threw up Valentines, and when I went through the check-out line there were these guys in front of me, and they had a twelve-pack of beer and four cheap, frozen pizzas. I thought about how that life is *so* far away!"

Feeling guilty that Miguel had given up cheap pizza and beer with the guys to be here with her, Lourdes grimaced. Thanking Miguel, she told him how much she loved the stuffed puppy and would save it for the baby.

The next day, Lourdes told Katie about the pink puppy.

Angela, close by, said, "My daddy gave me flowers. He gave me and mommy flowers and he gave Eli a truck. I gave mommy and daddy a picture we made in Sunday School. We made a picture of a heart, and then put our hand-prints under it, and our teacher wrote, '*You hold my heart in your hands.*'"

Katie looked at Angela with such tenderness and said, "Awwww. Very sweet. Your parents will take good care of your heart!"

Looking at Lourdes, Katie added, "I think that is so WISE of Jesse to do that! We spend far too much time asking young children if they have a boyfriend or girlfriend, and far too little time helping them discover who they are."

Hoping that someday she would discover who she really was, Lourdes smiled.

The weather turned misty and gray, almost as though the atmosphere was transitioning out the rainy cold of winter, but leaving enough lingering, chilled moisture that Lourdes wondered if spring would come.

Over the next few days, Miguel developed a cough, presumably from being out in the cold for too long. "Lourdes," Miguel said, "I need you to buy me some whiskey. My mom would mix whiskey and lemon juice, and it always helped me."

"Whiskey? You want me to go to a liquor store? I thought Mr. Dallas was against drinking because of his past employees."

Miguel answered, "I'm not going to get drunk. I just need something to settle my cough. Can you do that for me?"

Lourdes looked at him blankly.

"You have the habit of telling every person what you're doing, and why you're doing it. You don't need to do that. *Just go buy whiskey.* Okay?" he asked.

"Miguel, I'm not twenty-one years old. I can't buy stuff from a liquor store!"

"There's a place I know about and they won't check your license. All you have to do is go in and act like it's no big deal. Okay? No big deal."

Miguel had never asked for one single thing from her. She had to - wanted to - help him, even if it was something potentially illegal. What if they called the police and she had to go to jail? "I wish he just wanted a batch of chocolate chip cookies," she mumbled as she drove into the parking lot of the liquor store the next day.

Timidly, Lourdes walked inside. "Ummm," she said to the salesgirl, "I need to buy some whiskey, but he doesn't want to get drunk, so, do you have something like a 'whiskey Lite?'"

The girl's face contorted while she asked, "Whiskey Lite?"

"Yeah. Like they have Lite beer . . . do they make a whiskey Lite?"

Perplexed, the girl behind the counter shook her head. "Nope. Nothing like that," she said.

Lourdes began explaining what she was doing, and why she was doing it, "He has a cough and I need to buy some whiskey to mix it with lemon juice. It's for that."

The girl walked over to some *Jim Beam* and said, "I think this will work."

After buying the whiskey, without getting arrested, she decided to drive through *Dairy Queen* for a vanilla Coke. The *Dairy Queen* was right across the street from the liquor store, and Lourdes thought how funny it was that people seemed expressionless as they walked toward their addiction to liquor. She wondered if she had the same expressionless face as she went through the drive-thru to satisfy her addiction to vanilla Coke.

Miguel only had to work on Saturday if something special was needed. Lourdes and Miguel both enjoyed sleeping late now that sleeping in the same bed had become normal. They talked about buying a futon for the other bedroom, but because of the heating issue, they continued to share. Both wore thick layers of clothing and both were respectful of each other's privacy. They usually chatted a little while they lay in bed. The *Harry Potter* series they had been listening to was almost finished, and the TV they had been saving for would hopefully be purchased the beginning of March.

Although no one had given them a television set, people had been extremely generous to them. Sister Hessie let Lourdes pick out something from her *RV and Collectables* store. Lourdes found some matching plates and glassware, which made her feel like dining in the pink house was like feasting in a quaint cottage. Normally glassware wouldn't have that kind of emotional sway on people but for a pregnant Lourdes - it did.

This particular Saturday morning, Miguel was needed at work. Lourdes knew he still didn't feel well since the whiskey concoction hadn't fully cured the cough. Wanting to help him, she hopped in the rumbling truck, and they drove out to Archie Dallas Farms to feed a bunch of goats. Miguel turned into a beautiful pasture.

Goats were everywhere, standing beside a well-tended, but aging, barn. Miguel backed the truck close to a feeding spout. He stood on the back bumper of the truck, pulled the spout, and feed began to flow.

The spout stuck in the open position, and as feed barreled out, it missed the bucket spilling onto the ground. Miguel tried closing the spout, pushing it with all his might while Billy Goat horns scratched his bottom.

Lourdes sat inside the truck and laughed. Miguel really isn't a farm hand, she thought to herself. He seemed more precious in that moment than ever.

After Miguel fixed the problem and got back into the truck, Lourdes, still giggling, said, "I don't know if I tell you often enough how much I appreciate you! I appreciate how nice you are to me. I appreciate how hard you work to take care of us. I've never met anyone like you!"

Miguel blushed and shrugged off the compliment.

At church on Sunday, Lourdes told Katie the story of the goats scratching Miguel's bottom, adding, "He is such a good guy. I try to tell him, but I don't think he believes me."

Katie listened to the story and said, "A wise woman builds up her house, but a foolish one tears it down with her own hands.

I think you are wise in being quick with your words to build him up.

It's so easy to complain and find fault, but that just tears down the person you're living with . . . and it isn't very wise. I'd love to tell young brides how important it is to realize the power of your words and your moods!"

Not being a couple, Lourdes knew that didn't really apply to her and Miguel, but it did seem like good advice.

Sister Hessie walked to the piano of King's Community Church, veered left, corrected her course, and sat down on the bench. The songs were beginning to seem a little more familiar to Lourdes.

Aaron Anderson began by showing the model of a human brain. "Our brains are a gross, wormy-looking, handful of mass. If you looked at the brain intently, even with the most powerful microscope, you would never see the images of memory and feelings that cause us to love or hate or feel loved or hated.

It's those invisible brain functions that cause us to act and react the way we do.

Remember, it is what happens in the gray matter of your brain that really matters.

Guard your thoughts as much as you guard your money or anything else you treasure.

Encourage lovely thoughts, pure thoughts, thoughts that lead to hope and not depression.

You spend all day, every day...with yourself...inside your head. Make it a good day!"

Even though Lourdes had no experience with trying to manage her emotions, there was something uplifting about the thought.

The next week, Avy Faye needed another treatment. Lourdes pulled up to Crockett Elementary School were Avy was volunteering. "Your chariot awaits!" Lourdes said to a smiling Avy.

The weather was bad, but it was much worse in places not far from Memphis. To the north, they were having more ice. To the south and east, they had the possibility of tornadoes.

Since Lourdes didn't have any appointments for herself, she decided to go to a theatre showing dollar movies. The movie being so cheap meant she could treat herself to some popcorn and Sprite, which was something she hadn't done since her last day of work at the cinema.

De-Lovely, a movie about the life of Cole Porter, was a musical filled with songs that Lourdes had never heard, and it played to an almost empty theatre. After the movie, Lourdes continued to sit through the credits, which rolled while Cole Porter music played. Avy had an extra appointment today, and Lourdes preferred to listen to the music than sit in the hospital hallway.

Out of the corner of her eye, Lourdes noticed an older woman gently dancing in the aisle. She was wearing a large white hat with a flower on top. The woman clearly thought she was alone in the theatre. Lourdes didn't move out of fear of disrupting the dance.

Lourdes wondered what the woman with the wide-brimmed hat was thinking. Was she dancing with a long-lost love? Was she imagining herself surrounded by traces of friends at a glorious party?

There was something sacred and touching about the dance.

The lights in the theatre began to brighten. In vain, Lourdes tried to blend into the seats not wanting to destroy the moment.

The blazing reality of the present day stopped the woman, who spotted Lourdes, and quickly walked out.

With a whisper of curiosity, Lourdes's mind did a quick fast-forward into her future. Would she be an overwhelmed person like her aunt? Would she be a terrible mother like her own? Was there any chance she could be someone dancing with the memory of a contented life?

Not wanting to answer her own questions, she followed the woman out into the windy parking lot.

THE PANCAKE PIG-OUT

"Miguel, last night I dreamed I bought a forty-one thousand dollar hat!" Lourdes laughed, knowing the woman from the theatre had entered her dreamland.

He quipped back, "I hope you kept the receipt so we can return it!"

The first day of March started warm and spring-like, but merely a week later it was thirty-five degrees. Thankfully for Lourdes, the ice and snow were still fifty miles to the north, and she hoped it stayed there. This Texas girl had had enough cold weather. It was okay for a Tennessee Christmas, but she was wondering if they would ever have a Tennessee spring.

She wasn't experiencing too much pregnancy unpleasantness anymore, but she was showing a bit of a belly bump. The ultrasound picture was stuck onto the refrigerator, reminding Lourdes this was all too real.

Miguel's parents called often, continuing to want them to come home and move back. The more they called, the more Lourdes wondered if she would like living there. She thought they wanted the baby and Miguel to move home because they were anxious to replace Roy. Knowing she would be part of the package deal meant that once again she would land on the doorstep of someone required to take care of her.

For the first time in her life, she was living on her own – with Miguel as a roommate – and liked it.

After yet another phone call, Lourdes said, "I don't know Miguel. They seem a little . . ." She wanted to say 'pushy,' but having never met them, and because they were Miguel's parents, she said nothing, not wanting to be rude.

Not making Lourdes finish her sentence, Miguel said, "Let's just see what happens. I've told them we're going to stay here until after the baby comes. You like the doctors and the clinic. I like my job. I think you're really helping Avy and Katie. We're doing good here . . . for now."

Miguel occasionally talked about Roy with Lourdes, but the frequency and tone were changing. Distance from his old life seemed to help ease his grief.

The next Saturday, Lourdes drove Avy Faye and the kids to Memphis for a shopping trip at *Target*.

"I'm really glad you like to drive, Lourdes," Avy Faye said. "My energy level has been so low lately, and sometimes Jesse really frightens me the way he drives. Did I tell you the story about our car trip last summer?" Avy Faye gently laughed.

Lourdes shook her head. She loved the stories and conversation she had with Avy Faye on their trips to chemo. It wasn't a traditional way for women to spend time together, but it was special to them. They both said they hoped some day to go shopping at the mall and eat out for fun - instead of Jell-O at the hospital cafeteria.

"Last summer we drove to Virginia and during the times that Angela was awake she'd say, 'My stomach hurts. I might throw up. I might not.' And Eli would say, 'Oooooo. Sick-o.' In between those bouts of stimulating conversation, they would play wrestle-mania.

It was . . ." Avy just shook her head, unable to capture her feelings with words.

After a quick pause, Avy continued, "Jesse has quick instincts, and I think he assumes he could have been a sports car driver the way his eyes glaze over and he jockeys for position. He scares me to death sometimes!

I had to laugh, or well, cry. I said, 'Honey, I need more space between cars than this. Please, don't drive so close to everybody.'"

Lourdes giggled, "Jesse seems so laid back! That's really surprising."

Avy said, "He says he is *forced* to drive aggressively because everyone else does!

Anyway, I thought to myself, 'Ooooo. Sick-o. My stomach hurts. I might throw up. I might not.'"

Taking a quick look at a smiling Lourdes, Avy continued, "As much as I fretted, we got there and back safely. Angela didn't throw up. And on the very last night . . . as hard as being a tourist had been on all of us . . . Angela put her arms around Jesse and told him that she loved him. I thought how nice it must be for our Heavenly Father to hear us tell Him that we love Him, especially after a long, hard day of being a tourist on planet Earth."

Lourdes looked over at Avy and saw a sweet smile on her face.

Arriving at *Target*, Lourdes asked Avy if she had the energy to go inside. She answered, "Right now, I think I do!" Inside, other shoppers were leaving their buggies haphazardly in the middle of the aisle, not following the common rule of traffic.

Merging was the survival of the fittest.

Avy's energy quickly began to wane, so they picked up the items they needed and got back to the car.

Monday morning, Avy dropped Eli off at school, dropped Angela off with Katie, and went home to rest. "I think the trip to *Target* was more than she could do," Katie said quietly to Lourdes, not wanting Angela to hear.

Lourdes watched as Tucker worked on his new project, building a workshop in the back of the property. He and Katie worked together, step-by-step, with cooking and cleaning for the bed and breakfast. As for more construction, Katie told Lourdes she had had her fill, leaving the slowly progressing workshop to Tucker. "The biggest bonus of not helping build the workshop," Katie added, "is my eye has stopped twitching!"

Walking to the kitchen to grab Angela a snack, Lourdes asked Katie, "Have you ever noticed that your cats follow you from room to room? I thought dogs did that, not cats."

"Macey Gray sees herself as a cross between a dog and a favorite child. She follows me everywhere I go. Then Brownie Boo doesn't want to be left out and follows, really I think out of fear."

"Fear of what?" asked Lourdes.

"Fear of everything. Brownie is frightened of life in general, which, come to think of it, is also the human condition."

The two women looked down at the cats. Brownie, who must have been the chapter president for PETI (Pets for the Ethical Treatment of Insects) was glaring at Macey, who was toying with a bug. Katie got a tissue and saved the little bug, putting it outside.

After rescuing the insect, Katie, Lourdes and Angela started cleaning the kitchen. Angela was more interested in seeing if there was any more sugary goodness that she could have.

While scrubbing the sink, Katie said, "I got an email from Julie yesterday and she asked about you."

"Oh, that's sweet. How are they doing?" Lourdes asked while eating a cookie along with Angela.

"Caleb has had one cold after another. I think this time of year and the weather changing just makes everyone's nose runny." Laughing, Katie added, "She went to a friend's house for a visit, and she put him down for a nap. Julie said he woke up on the wrong side of the pack-n-play, so they had to go home."

Back in the kitchen, Brownie had been alerted to danger and flew through the air, heading toward Katie and Tucker's bedroom area.

Watching Brownie with a laugh, Katie said, "You know, I really can't judge the poor kitty. When CNN met my genetic disposition toward fear . . . it was like . . . KABOOM . . . I started to fight my own War on Terror, really my own war against being TERRIFIED!

One day, though, I was praying and I felt like the Lord told me that 'fear is a lie.' It sort of took me aback . . . the root of my fear is basically that I'm afraid God won't be there to answer my prayer, or help me, or that in some way God will leave me in ruin.

So I'm choosing to fight my own war against terror, because it's easy for me to KABOOM . . . TERROR," she finished with a smiling wink.

Lourdes smiled, although it was a fake attempt to hide her own struggle with anxiety.

Mid-March brought St. Patrick's Day. It was spectacular weather, clear skies with temperatures in the seventies. While most of the world was having fun picking out a green outfit or drinking a glass of green beer, Lourdes and Avy were on their way to Memphis for another round of chemo.

Lourdes asked, "Did I tell you my dream last night?"

Avy Faye laughed, "You and your dreams! What was it this time?"

"I dreamed my name was Jan Williams, and I'd gone back in time to the French Revolution. I was really good at tracking, so I was able to hide in the woods really well."

"Tracking . . . in the woods?" Avy asked skeptically.

Lourdes laughed, "Well, the woods were dark but had a beautiful blue hue, so it was quite pleasant. I met some other people who were hiding, and they asked me the secret question to see if I was on their side. They asked, 'What is the opposite of Rock Hudson?'"

Avy interrupted, "The French Revolution and Rock Hudson! I'm really surprised you've even heard of Rock Hudson."

"I know it doesn't make sense! Well, in my dream it did," Lourdes chuckled.

Avy asked, "So what is the opposite of Rock Hudson?"

"I don't know! I woke up. And I'd really like to know the answer to that, too."

Avy said in her soft voice, "Sometimes, when I talk to you, well, I just have to laugh."

On the drive home from the chemo appointment, the mood in the car was decidedly dark. Avy scratched her head, causing a lot of hair to fall out. Looking at her hair forlornly, she rolled down the window and let it blow out of the car. "Maybe some birds will make a nest out of it," she said softly.

Unprepared for situations of this gravity, Lourdes drove wordlessly. But after thinking about it a minute, she said, "You know. I think you're going to be just fine. You're going to get well. Well, that's what I think." For Lourdes there honestly wasn't a hint of a thought of a different outcome. How could Avy Faye die? Surely, God wouldn't let that happen.

Avy Faye smiled, "I like it when you drive me to my appointments. Sometimes I feel like I have to comfort my friends, and I really don't always have the energy to do that."

"Seriously, I think you're going to be okay!" Lourdes said, convinced.

"You went and bought a hair shaver and cut Miguel's hair, right?" Avy asked.

"Yep. I shave it every week or two. It's super easy."

Avy took a serious breath and said, "Let's go to the pink house, so you can shave mine a lot shorter. Do you mind doing that now?"

"Sure! Let's do it," Lourdes answered easily.

Avy continued, "I think the kids won't notice it falling out if it is shorter. Then in a few weeks, I can get a wig. I don't have the wig from before, but I know where to get one. I just really don't want to worry the kids."

"We'll go straight to my house. Let's do it outside, so we can leave your hair on the ground, and the birds can build their nest.

It will be the finest nest around! The envy of all the other birds!" Lourdes said dramatically.

They cut her hair outside, underneath the thick oak tree so the birds could easily find the soft nesting material for their babies.

Avy Faye looked beautiful with a short afro. Her complexion was still a creamy milk chocolate, with no hint of the toxic chemicals floating through her body.

"You are so lucky!" commented Lourdes. "Your head is perfectly shaped. Mine is kind of flat on the backside of the top. I wouldn't look nearly as nice as you do."

"Oh, Lourdes," Avy said with a hint of a smile.

The next day Avy told Lourdes that Eli and Angela barely noticed her shorter hair. Jesse noticed it and told her she was still the most beautiful girl he had ever seen.

Easter fell on the first Sunday of April this year. Katie's mom and dad would be coming for an Easter visit and staying the following week. King's Community Church had an Easter pancake breakfast they called 'The Pancake Pig-Out.'

This particular Easter morning was splendid, the temperature was a moderate sixty degrees. The sky was a perfect match of blue dyed onto many of the colored Easter eggs. The cooperative weather brought the added bonus of the children's Easter Egg Hunt.

Lourdes and Miguel arrived at church the same time as Katie and Tucker, who brought with them Katie's parents, Cracker and Ginny Philpott. Ginny, who was wearing an elegant white silk hat with its brim slightly sloping over her eyebrows, greeted Lourdes and Miguel with a genuine warmth.

"Wow! You look wonderful!" Lourdes said.

With a grin, Ginny primped her hair.

"You look lovely, Lourdes. How are you feeling?" asked Ginny.

Lourdes, who was wearing a colorful, loose-fitting maternity dress she had picked up from the thrift store, said, "Fine. Really good," she nodded happily.

"Katie keeps me up on all the happenings in Kingsville, so she's been keeping me posted about you two. I am glad you're still here," Ginny said with a hug.

Polly wandered up to get her hug from Ginny. She said, "Y'all come on in and get a plate. They're making fresh pancakes and there are lots of side dishes, too. I made some really gooey cinnamon rolls." Waving her hand for effect, she added, "Don't y'all love the word 'gooey?' Gooey is just another word for yummy, sticky, comfort food." Polly was always animated and happy, but somehow describing food heightened her sense of joy.

Ginny added, "When I think of comfort food, I think of meat loaf with mac and cheese."

Lourdes said, "I think of potato soup. Lately, if I'm not feeling well, Miguel makes me potato soup. And if we have any left, we take it to Avy Faye or Big Momma."

In unison, Polly and Ginny asked, "Is Avy Faye coming today?" Their heads began to twist around to see if they could spot anyone from her family.

Ginny asked Lourdes, "Do you see her every day? Katie told me you're helping out by watching the kids, driving her around, and doing their laundry."

"Well, I pick-up the laundry twice a week. I do see Angela pretty much every day, but lately Katie and Tucker and I have switched out taking the kids home. So, I don't see Avy every day. I think Big Momma might, though. She goes over to stay with her a lot."

Right on cue, Eli and Angela came running toward the chatting women. The children were beautifully dressed and each had a basket for collecting plastic egg-filled goodies. Eli carried a wicker basket, and Angela had a pink basket in the shape of a bunny with a polka-dot collar. Both baskets had green plastic grass spilling out over the sides. Jesse wasn't far behind them, walking toward the group to give everyone a hug.

"Good to see you!" Jesse said to Ginny with a robust laugh. "Aren't you glad the weather is better than the last time you were in Kingsville? I think you left as soon as you could after the Christmas ice storm."

"Cracker had his doctor appointments," answered Ginny. "The doctors always seem to think he is doing fine, but then want to see him again in a few months. I don't know why they say someone is fine, but then set up more appointments. I think he would do better if they left him alone.

He needs new hearing aids, but he said he has one foot in the grave and doesn't want to spend the money on upgrading them. I have to yell myself hoarse trying to get his attention!"

With antsy feet, quite ready to be in the line of children who were just moments away from running and shoving their way to finding chocolate treasures, Eli and Angela asked, "Can we go now?"

"Okay," answered Jesse. "Remember don't run over any of the little-little kids. Try not to get grass stains on your new clothes, and remember that if you don't find enough Easter eggs, they'll be plenty more later." Eli and Angela bolted off while Jesse shouted, "I'll be right there!"

"Is Avy Faye coming today?" The question was posed simultaneously from Lourdes, Ginny and Polly.

Jesse, with a solemn smile, shook his head. "Big Momma is going to stay with her this morning."

"Well, there is plenty of really good food in there, so go fix yourself a plate. It's already been blessed!" Polly, who orchestrated the church functions with the skill of a maestro, made sure food was blessed early so eating could begin at will.

"I'm going to go watch the kids, and then we'll be right in." Jesse hugged all the ladies standing around, wandering away to watch the hunt.

Lourdes and Miguel went inside to taste the pancakes, the gooey cinnamon rolls and whatever else might be offered, which were set up in several different stations. Most of the men were cooks at the pancake station, which was getting a lot of action. There was a station of drinks of juice and coffee, and lastly there was a table with homemade bakery items.

They found Polly's cinnamon rolls, and while they were there noticed the chocolate chip mini-muffins. Polly's cinnamon rolls were exceptional, but there was something so intoxicating about the mini-muffins that you could only eat three or four before you reached the legal limit.

"These people sure know how to eat," Miguel said as he took another bite of pancakes. "But I could show them how to make good rice, beans, and tamales. My mom's recipe has been handed down from a long time back, and they're the best in town! Did you ever eat at our food truck?"

"No, I never did. I know about it, but didn't you usually take it to construction sites? Did you cook, too?" asked Lourdes with her mouth full of food.

"Not really cooked so much. Mostly, I delivered the food and fixed things that broke. But I imagine I could cook good if I wanted to," he said with a sly smile.

Lourdes gave him a playful nudge and said, "Well, I KNOW you can make a good comforting bowl of potato soup!"

Deciding to watch the egg hunt, Lourdes and Miguel took their plates outside.

The Easter eggs had been scattered inside a large square which was spray-painted onto the grass. The various families stood bunched around the perimeter waiting for the signal to start.

With the sound of an air horn, the children were off, marching from all sides of the square, looking like ants picking up the oval-shaped prizes. Luckily, it was a kindly crowd, and even the little kids were able to grab eggs while the older kids scurried toward the middle of the square.

Within mere minutes, the festivities were over as all the candy-filled eggs were collected, and everyone was inside eating pancakes.

The Easter service at King's Community Church began with the children doing a special sign language song that looked more like Polly trying to do yoga, but it was energetic and sweet.

Pastor Aaron stood up and walked behind the podium. With his usual commanding calm, he began with a broad grin, "Today is Easter Sunday, and I want to talk about Jesus."

Stepping away from the podium, he continued, "Some say Jesus is only a myth. But just thirty years after the death of Jesus, the Roman Emperor Nero was putting Christians to death in the coliseum. To face that kind of death, well, Jesus wasn't a myth to any of them. Men who knew Jesus and witnessed his life, death, and resurrection died violent deaths because they wouldn't deny him. Jesus was no mere story to them. *He was a current event.*"

Pastor Aaron held his hands out, as though he were holding up something personal to the congregation. "You've heard John 3:16 before, but what does this beautiful verse say?"

He calmly breathed out, "*You* are loved."

He paused. "By believing in Jesus, God's only son, *you* will have eternal life."

Another deep breath, and he said, "Jesus didn't come to condemn *you.*"

Looking around the room with a galvanized gaze, he said, "Jesus came to save *you.*"

Lourdes took a mental pause. Saved? Would she be included in the private club up in heaven?

Never chosen . . . never feeling like she belonged . . . was she loved by God?

Was God accepting of her?

Her little mind-wandering trail must have only lasted a blink because she resumed listening as Pastor Aaron said, "Thankfully,

God reaches out to us. If you were to make a T-chart and on one side write every good thought, or every bad thought, or activity you've ever had - and on the opposite side of that list write only the name Jesus, well, you can put an 'X' over your successes and failures, and you can know it is only believing in Jesus that puts you in relationship with God. Jesus alone stands."

He held up left hand, running it from high to low indicating his list-of-life. He held his right hand in a cupped position as though he was holding the name of Jesus. Then his left hand made a large 'X' over his invisible list - while his right hand, holding the name of Jesus - held firm.

"I can have a right relationship with God not because I am able to be good enough, but because I believe in Jesus."

Looking around the room, answering unspoken questions, he added, "Of course behavior matters. Should we do whatever we want just because of God's grace? Of course not. Behavior has consequences not only in this world but in the world to come." Leaning forward, with his hand cupped to his mouth as though telling a secret, said, "You want a good stock tip for your long-term, eternal rewards? Follow God."

He grinned, continuing, "The interesting thing is," he paused, "the more you experience following the ways of God - the more you want to follow Him. Your 'want-to-do' joins that journey and matures along with you.

We live in this world as a prism reflecting the Spirit of God," he held out his flat hand as though holding an invisible object, "taking the pure white light from God and dispersing it into multi-colors."

Lourdes envisioned something like the pyramid in front of the Louvre - now small enough to fit into his hand, clear, but occasionally blazing with brilliant color.

"We reflect God's love, joy, peace, patience, kindness, goodness, gentleness, faithfulness and self-control." While naming each characteristic, Pastor Aaron took his hand, touched the invisible prism, and began individually flinging those traits into space as though they were shooting stars - now illuminating a dark night-time sky.

It was true. Lourdes knew she wasn't in Kingsville because of moral finger-pointing. It was the artful persuasion of joy and kindness flowing from these fine people, wooing her to a better place.

Pastor Aaron continued, "Discovering the delight of honoring God with our thoughts, words and actions - we find a life we can feel good about."

He smiled gently, shifted his feet and held onto the podium with both hands.

Something in that moment must have been exceptionally real to him because he started singing, almost in tears, "In Christ alone . . . my hope is found."

He didn't have a good singing voice. It was rough and broken. But his raw and honest tone was something Lourdes hadn't known before.

Pastor Aaron ended the service with a simple prayer of thanks.

Touched by the idea *she* was invited to join with God and it was her choice to believe or reject, Lourdes looked at Miguel and whispered, "I believe that."

Miguel nodded his head and whispered back, "I believe that, too."

The tiniest sliver of hope that she could be loved inched into her soul.

Sister Hessie sauntered up to the piano, and they all touchingly sang, *Amazing Grace.*

It seemed to Lourdes as though King's Community Church had never seen their pastor so openly moved, the congregation disbanded, subdued.

Even though they were invited to Safehaven for lunch, Lourdes and Miguel decided to go home for a good Sunday afternoon nap.

As they said their goodbyes to the fine people of King's Community Church, Miguel pushed his luck, sought out whatever was left of the intoxicating chocolate chip mini-muffins, and grabbed the last few for the road.

TABLE TALK

The pink house had become a home for Lourdes. Although not a place that most girls would be proud to call home, for Lourdes it was a delightful dwelling. The only thing that bugged her about it was the condition of the bathroom floor.

The dingy, peeling linoleum around the toilet was taking its toll on the early-onset nesting phase of her pregnancy. Miguel, sent to ask if Mr. Dallas minded if they changed out the flooring, returned that evening with the news they could do as they pleased.

"I think 'peel and stick' linoleum squares are cheerful and cheap," Lourdes remarked while they were at the *Habitat for Humanity ReStore* in Memphis. The shop was located in an old warehouse where she and Miguel regularly found good bargains. The selection wasn't huge on the peel and stick squares, but they found a few matching boxes of French blue with a creamy-yellow pattern that Lourdes liked.

Having no paying guests at Safehaven, Tucker said he would come over on Saturday and help Miguel tear out the old floor and install the new one. The room being so small, they expected it to be a quick job. However, Lourdes had learned something about Miguel - he lacked the ability to determine how much time it would take to do anything. If Miguel said he would be home in twenty minutes, she knew it would probably be forty-five. If Miguel said it would take an hour to do a project, she knew it would likely take three. Since this project was thought to take a morning, she knew she would be lucky if they finished the same day.

Surprisingly to Lourdes, the demolition phase was fast. But disgusted by the look and smell of the torn-out linoleum, she waved goodbye to the guys and headed over to Safehaven. Katie answered the door wearing loose fitting, white Capri pants.

Katie looked a little bedraggled, without her usual cheery disposition. "I know," she said looking down at her pants, "these pants are not fit for human consumption, because they oddly make me look like a hobbit."

Not being someone to start a conversation with, "You look awful," Lourdes simply smiled and walked inside.

"I feel terrible. I am so tired of not getting over this cold, or allergies, or whatever this dratted thing is," Katie slumped toward the couch and fell into its welcoming arms. "I've tried everything, but I think I'm going to break down and go to the doctor, which I absolutely HATE to do!"

She breathed heavily out of her mouth since her nostrils were partially out-of-order. "I'm going to call on Monday and see when I can get an appointment. I guess I'm lucky we don't have any guests this weekend - I'd have to put on my happy face and greeted and cooked."

Sitting straighter, she looked at Lourdes and continued, "I hate to complain, but I guess that's all I've been doing since you got here. How are you doing, Lourdes?"

"I'm feeling pretty good, and I'm sorry that you're not! I just wondered if it was okay if I hung out here with you while they're working on my bathroom."

The two women settled in to watch some television. Katie lay on the couch while Lourdes got them something to drink. It felt good to be taking care of Katie, who had done so much for her.

Around lunch time, Lourdes made turkey with avocado sandwiches for everyone, and leaving Katie to eat alone, she took the rest to the pink house.

"How are they coming along?" Katie asked when Lourdes returned half-an-hour later.

"They're about half-way finished. They have the old floor out and have string and chalk lines down for installing the new squares. They have a couple of rows already in place. It already looks so much better!"

"This morning, Tucker told me he thought they'd be finished by lunch, but he can't judge time – at all – it usually takes him twice as long as he thinks it will."

Lourdes laughed, "No way! Miguel is just like that! When he tells me how long something is going to take I start adding time. Is that a guy thing?"

"Well, I don't know, but I guess it is OUR guys' thing," Katie laughed, then coughed.

At the end of the day, the cheerful and cheap linoleum squares were in place. Mr. Dallas, who Lourdes rarely saw, came by to inspect the improvement.

"Looks good . . . looks good," he nodded his head in approval. "You're a good man, Miguel. Good man." Mr. Dallas chuckled, patted Miguel on the back, hugged Lourdes, and went on his way.

Church attendance took a decided hit the next day. Katie and Tucker stayed home, as did Lourdes and Miguel. Lourdes later learned that Avy and Jesse stayed home, too, although Jesse did drop off Angela and Eli for Sunday School, mostly because it was almost impossible to keep Eli from handing out bulletins.

The weather was warm and muggy. Now that it was nearing the end of April, the heat and humidity would only be rising.

Katie called for a doctor's appointment and got one for Wednesday morning at ten-thirty. Because of a change in her insurance, which had dropped her previous doctor from their network, she made her appointment with an unknown physician from the list of providers.

Tucker and Big Momma were tapped for the job of caring for Angela and Eli so that Avy Faye, Polly and Lourdes could take Katie into town.

Avy Faye didn't have a lot of energy, but she was sick and tired of feeling sick and tired. Wanting to do, or think, about something else for a change, she asked to go along. Polly never missed a party and this was shaping up to be a good one, despite Avy and Katie's tiredness.

Polly drove her large SUV while Lourdes sat in the front seat with her. "It feels so strange to go to Memphis with Avy and not be driving!" Lourdes remarked, turning around and smiling at Avy Faye.

"After I finish with my appointment, I'll call you so you can come back and pick me up. Then we can go for lunch at *Belle's*," Katie told the group as they dropped her off at a large, impersonal clinic with her new doctor's office inside.

Polly drove them to Castle Road Mall for a little shopping therapy. Lourdes knew Avy wouldn't have enough energy for a full shopping day, but even just a few hours away from thoughts of cancer might seem like a vacation to her.

After only a short time of walking the mall, Katie called Polly to come pick her up. Within thirty minutes, they were all sitting around a table at *Belle's*.

The restaurant was located inside a small boutique filled with antiques and gift items. The dining tables were round with white cloths draping to the floor. The chairs looked as though they were out of an ice cream parlor. Luckily, there were plump cushions to make an extended conversation more comfortable for any size bottom. The place felt elegant yet still friendly.

The menu was filled with marvelous sounding soups and salads, all of which were filled with 'cream of' something, promising high-fat deliciousness.

"What did the doctor say?" asked Lourdes after they were settled.

"Wait . . . let's order and I'll tell you," Katie said, as a young, friendly waitress walked their way.

"How are you all today?" the waitress asked as she put down drink napkins in front of them.

"Well, the doctor seems to think I'm fine," Katie answered, uncharacteristically cross. Wisely, the waitress let the comment slide and took the drink order with the promise of a quick return.

Polly asked, "So darlin', what on earth happened at that doctor's office?"

It was clear to Lourdes, and everyone else at the table, that Katie was indignant.

"Well." Katie took a breath as though she would be talking for a few minutes before she could come up for air again. "At the doctor's office, a young nurse wearing blue scrubs opened the door and called out, 'Katie Barkley.'

I dutifully followed along and the nurse politely asked me, 'How are you today?'

I said, 'I've been better, but thanks for asking.'

Then she said, 'Let's get your weight. If you'll just stand on the scales for me, please.'

Normally, I'm quite compliant, but I looked at those scales, and I turned to that young girl and said, 'I weigh the same as I always do. It's in my records my previous doctor sent you.'"

Lourdes and the other ladies laughed out loud.

"I'm not sure what I was thinking," Katie continued. "I guess with my lack of sleep, and not feeling like myself, something just rose up out of me like an unpleasant, evil twin. Anyway, the young nurse didn't know if I was kidding and looked at me weird.

So I held my ground and said, 'My weight is on a need-to-know basis, and I don't think we need to know that today.'"

Lourdes was now smiling so hard she thought it might become a permanent expression.

Katie said, "She just looked at me and didn't move. So I said, 'Well, I'm here because my throat kinda hurts, I don't feel good, and I don't think it is because of how much I weigh.'" Katie's tone was defiant.

Lourdes could only imagine what the nurse must have been thinking.

"I guess she didn't get paid enough to argue with patients," Katie continued, "so she nodded her head and said, 'Okay, well, come on into this room and I do need to take your blood pressure.'

After a few minutes of me sitting on the examining table, fiddling with the white covering paper, the doctor came in."

Lourdes noticed Katie started fiddling with her napkin, possibly as illustration.

"He ran a strep test, which was negative, he checked out my chest and ears and nose and throat. He didn't ask about my weight. Then he asked, 'Where exactly do you hurt?'

I said I have a cough, but I don't have a lot of specific symptoms. I just don't feel good.

The doctor, quite unwisely, – maybe from having a bad day himself or maybe having a bad impression of me because I didn't want to get on the scale – flippantly asked, 'Then why exactly are you here?'

I said, 'I don't feel good, and I'm tired of not feeling good.'" Katie's voice took on a heightened volume of exasperation. Lourdes moved her hand to cover her mouth, hiding her amusement, and wondered what Katie must have sounded like to the doctor.

"He said, 'I don't find anything wrong with you, but if you get any worse be sure to come back.' Then he turned to his nurse and added, 'Make sure to note that in her file.'

I think he just added that last part just to cover himself in case I turned out to have a serious ailment and could have sued him."

Even Avy, who was not given to laughing at someone's misery, got a soul-cleansing chuckle from the story.

Katie told them she thought it wasn't likely she would ever return to him, and it just reminded her how much she didn't like going to the doctor unless it was an emergency. She said she felt if he knew her, then he would know she wouldn't be there unless she felt really, really bad.

The waitress returned with the drinks and bread for the table. Polly picked up a breadstick, dipped it in olive oil, and looking adoringly at the bread said, "One bite of this will be a life-altering experience."

After the meals were ordered, Katie said, "When I was sitting in the waiting room, I heard a woman talking to whoever she was with, and she said that someone's baby had gotten out of the house. Whoever was watching the baby had to chase after it, but she had to run slowly because her uterus was slipping down. When she called the doctor he told her that your uterus dropping out isn't a medical emergency!"

The appalled expressions on the women's faces said everything they thought about that situation. Not a medical emergency? If that wasn't an emergency, then Lourdes didn't know what else could be!

"I'm guessing the doctor was a guy," noted Katie.

Changing the subject, Avy Faye asked Polly, "How are Charlotte and Savannah?"

Polly put down her bread and said, "Savannah is still working in Nashville. Charlotte, well, she hasn't exactly said she's having problems, but sometimes I wonder if she and Adam are having troubles. Adam doesn't share her energy and enthusiasm for spending money. But I do think he loves her," she paused, "in spite of her spoiled faults."

The conversation halted while the food was served.

Lourdes then told them all about the old wooden rocking chair, which had a calming creak in it every time she rocked down, that Miguel had brought home so she could rock the baby.

Polly piped back in, "Hey, y'all, did you know that Chrissy Long is living with that guy from the highway maintenance? But she is always on the phone or internet with two other guys. When I asked her about that she said, 'I don't like all the junk you have to put up with if you do the commitment thing.'"

Katie said, "I think the culture is against married couples. I feel like it is my job to help Julie and Luke succeed because the world is pretty much against them!"

Avy chimed in, "On TV the other day, I heard *Larry the Cable Guy* say 'a guy wouldn't sleep with an ugly woman.' I mean . . . really . . . is a guy being willing to sleep with you the measure of acceptance we should be striving for? I sure wouldn't want Angela to EVER think that way!" Her naturally quiet voice was more animated than normal.

Lourdes winced a little.

Polly said, "I know! I heard that at some Ivy League college, Yale maybe, the guys rated the freshman girls by how drunk they'd have to be to sleep with them. That's our future lawyers, CEO's, and presidents thinking that way!" Her face scowled and she whispered, "It's a sad state of affairs when our supposed best and brightest are no more evolved than *Larry the Cable Guy!*"

Lourdes could tell the group was about the change the subject, but had a question. "Don't you think that most women just don't want to be alone?"

The table was quiet for a moment. Polly gently said, "Honey, nobody wants to be alone. But you can feel lonely even if you're married and surrounded by people. Or you can feel at peace - even if you're alone."

Katie must have known what Lourdes was thinking, and reaching over she put her hand on top of Lourdes's. "Without a doubt, being a single parent has to be the hardest thing. Honestly, life is easier when you have someone to share your joys with - your experiences with - your bills with - your troubles with - but, never forget that God is the only one whose love satisfies our soul. That's true for *everyone* at this table."

Lourdes nodded her head, only wishing that were true.

"Hey," Avy Faye said, turning to talk to Katie, "Eli told me that Tucker is going to lead the prayer in church on Sunday. I don't think I've ever heard him speak before."

"No, he doesn't like to do things in public." Katie laughed, "When he was a little boy, standing in front of his church to get baptized, the preacher asked him if he wanted to accept Jesus' gift of forgiveness, but he was so nervous he didn't say anything and only sort of nodded his head. Since then he has never wanted to speak in church."

Polly said, "Isn't it funny how stuff like that stays with us? Even if it is fifty years later, it can still feel like yesterday.

I just wish we could all go to every school kid and let them know that this only lasts a few years - people grow up and change. And don't let the kids around you bully or bother you so much, because afterwards you don't see them anymore - unless you carry them around with you in your mind."

A text came in from Atufftt. Lourdes quietly said aloud, "Oh. Atufftt!" Lourdes texted in repy to Miguel that they'd be on their way home soon.

"Atufftt?" Polly asked with a laugh.

"Yeah," Lourdes looked up from her phone. "It's Miguel. I must have put it in wrong, and I never did fix it to Archie Dallas Farms. When I see 'Atufftt' pop-up, it makes me laugh."

To finish the random conversation, Polly said, "Jane told me they had taken the boys to the lake. They could see a boat that was thirty yards ahead of them, pulling a naked man, who was standing on one ski!"

"What?" Katie said as she dropped her fork onto her plate.

"Yeah!" Polly continued, "And she said they were so enthralled with that man's bottom they didn't realize that their cousin, who they were pulling, had fallen into the lake!"

With the image of the water skier's naked bum heading into the sunset, Polly, with a wave of her hand, announced that lunch was her treat.

"Thanks, Polly," Avy Faye said, forcing a smile as she pushed her bowl a few inches forward, her expression painfully worn out.

Something about how Avy looked made Lourdes cringe.

AVY GOES ON

"Have you had any crazy dreams lately?" Avy Faye asked Lourdes as they were driving to Memphis for their doctors' appointments a week after the luncheon.

The weather was fair, which was Lourdes's favorite driving environment.

"Well," Lourdes gave a little giggle, "This morning, I dreamed that I was talking to somebody, and I guess they were cussing a lot because I kept hearing beep . . . beep, like on TV when the network is blocking bad words. Anyway, I woke up, and it was Miguel's alarm clock beeping. I guess he was super tired - normally he wakes up with the first beep."

Avy Faye laughed softly. "I hear Katie is feeling better."

Lourdes nodded, and said, "She still doesn't know what was wrong, but her energy is just about back to normal."

Avy asked, "How is Miguel enjoying his job?"

"Mr. Dallas is the best! He has been telling Miguel that he should go get training to work on airplane engines at the airport in Memphis. Apparently, it pays really good."

"Is he interested in doing that?"

"I never knew it about Miguel, but his dream job is to be a pilot. So working around airplanes would be really awesome. Well, not right now, or, not here, but, maybe someday." Lourdes changed the subject. "Were you tired after we got home from lunch in Memphis?"

"Yeah, I was. But I figure this is my life, and I'm going to enjoy it! I'm glad I went." Avy Faye's voice was slightly faded.

Lourdes took her eyes off the road, just for a moment, to get a fresh appraisal of Avy, who must have felt Lourdes's glance. Avy looked back with an affirming smile.

The ladies didn't talk anymore until they reached the hospital for Avy's appointment, then Lourdes drove herself to the clinic for her check-up.

Both women had a normal day at the doctor's office, and then they both enjoyed Jell-O at the cafeteria. "I found an ad while I was thumbing through a magazine back in the waiting area, and I thought of Miguel." Avy handed a crumpled, dog-eared magazine over to Lourdes, pointing to a particular spot. "It's about becoming an airplane mechanic. Mr. Dallas is right. The Memphis airport stays busy, and I thought he might want more information about doing something like that."

"Oh! Thanks! I'll show him." Lourdes stuffed the magazine into her already bulging purse.

"I need to come back the middle of June," Avy said between slurps of Jell-O. "Just some routine tests to check my progress."

"Well," Lourdes said, "I have to start coming in every three weeks, then every two weeks, and then once a week until the baby comes.

You know, I think I'm glad they don't do an ultrasound to see if the baby is a boy or girl. I know they would do things if they thought it was necessary, but, thankfully, everything is going normally. It feels old-fashioned not to know," she said with a slight shrug of her shoulders.

Avy laughed. "It's funny the things we take for granted - like knowing if you're going to have a boy or girl. That was unheard of a generation ago." Avy sighed. "I'm kind of tired, let's go home."

"Like I always say - your chariot awaits!"

The drive between Memphis and Kingsville seemed short now that Lourdes had driven it so many times. They were never in Memphis during peak traffic times. Lourdes was so cautious that Avy was never afraid.

"I rode into Memphis with Jesse the other day and I had forgotten how frightened I am with him behind the wheel. He still weaves in and out of traffic claiming that he has to keep up with the flow of traffic, and then if traffic speeds up, he zooms up, too. I kept pulling down on the handle above my door like it was some sort of an emergency brake!"

Lourdes laughingly said, "Oh, I know! I think the world would be a better place if there were only women drivers. I think we drive more calmly."

Avy's gentle laugh was followed by a quiet, "I don't even know the last time I drove."

After that Lourdes stopped talking because Avy Faye seemed sickly-green. Gentle music from James Taylor replaced any conversation.

A few weeks later, according to Eli, the temperature would reach ninety degrees. This was unpleasant news for Lourdes, who was finding the eighties nearly intolerable for the pink house.

No one was more excited for the end of school than little Angela. She knew she would start Kindergarten in August, and summer vacation brought her that much closer to running with the big kids.

Katie suggested the kids, with Lourdes, spend most of their summer weekdays at Safehaven.

Every morning, Lourdes brought her ever-expanding belly over to take care of Eli and Angela where they would walk down to the top of the driveway and get the mail out of the Safehaven mailbox. This time of year, she was accompanied by a skipping Angela and carefree, yellow butterflies.

Tomorrow, Lourdes would be taking Angela on her first trip to the dentist. Angela was a little apprehensive about going, but she tended to be a little anxious about things so everyone considered it typical behavior.

Sure enough, the following day, Angela was anxious and quiet. Lourdes played *Sesame Street* music in the car, singing along to keep Angela calm. "Hey, Angie, here we are!" Lourdes said overly cheerful, trying to convince Angela this was a good thing.

Eli said, "They have lots of good stuff to play with there. They have video games and TV." The office was whimsical and brilliantly colorful. Lourdes signed in at the front desk, soon a friendly young girl wearing a *Dora the Explorer* smock said, with a melodic lilt in her voice, "Angela Blue, we are ready for you."

Bravely, Angela followed. Thirty minutes later, she bounced out. Lourdes paid the invoice with a check from Avy.

In the car after the appointment, Angela turned to Eli and loudly pronounced, "He DID NOT take out my heart and check it for bones!"

Eli seemed very amused.

When they arrived back at Safehaven, Lourdes found Jane and her three-year-old son, Samuel, had dropped by for a short visit with Katie.

Eli and Angela were somber after they walked in and saw Samuel crying. Ice was being applied to the back of his hand.

Lourdes knew little kids never like to see other little kids crying. There is something contagious about it, somewhat like a virus.

"What happened?" asked Lourdes.

"A bird bit me!" wailed Samuel.

Jane looked at Lourdes and mouthed the word, 'wasp.'

"Oh, I'm sorry. When you feel a little better do you want to play with Eli and Angela?"

Trying to help, Katie said, "Eli, tell Samuel your new joke."

Eli had just begun the fine art of joke-telling. And in case any audience member missed the punch line, he would say, "Get it?" which was the cue to laugh.

"Why did the chicken cross the road?" Eli asked.

All the adults admitted they didn't know.

"Because he had a diaper on his head! Get it?"

After the appropriate amount of laughter, Eli added, "I made that one up!"

Angela wanted in on the attention. She held up a toothbrush the dentist had just given her. "Do you want me to make this disappear?"

All the adults happily nodded.

She made wild and elaborate hand gestures, while saying, "ABRACADABRA, I'll make my toothbrush disappear." Then looking at everyone, she said, "Okay, now, CLOSE YOUR EYES!"

The group complied while she stuffed the toothbrush into the couch.

"Okay, now, OPEN YOUR EYES!"

There was applause from the adults, while a cheating Eli, who had not closed his eyes, picked the toothbrush out from behind the couch cushion.

"You cheated! You didn't close your eyes!" Angela angrily shouted.

"Well, I squinted," Eli said.

The day had gone swiftly for Lourdes. She dropped the kids off at Big Momma's house, a small, one-story, white brick house with black shutters built in the 1960's, which was aging poorly from years of neglect.

Greeting them at the door, Big Momma said, "Avy said that you do her laundry, and that I should get you the basket of clothes. Can you do them today?"

"Of course! Normally, Jesse's been bringing them to me at Katie's house, but it's just as easy for me to pick them up here."

Big Momma and Lourdes each carried a basket of laundry to the car, with Eli and Angela walking along beside them. On top of a pile of clothes was a soft, white, calf-length nightgown. There were small pink roses sewn onto the top.

When Angela noticed the nightgown, she proudly said, "We gave that to Mom for Mother's Day."

"Then I'll be sure to wash it very carefully," Lourdes answered as Eli opened the car door for them.

Back at the pink house, Lourdes started the clothes. Just a couple of minutes later, Lourdes heard the rumble of Miguel's work truck. The familiar sound always made her feel delighted.

Immediately after Miguel came inside, he remembered a bag of vegetables that Mr. Dallas sent home for them and told Lourdes he had to run back out to the truck. Lourdes put on her flip-flops to walk outside with him.

He smiled and said, "Are those steel-toed shoes?"

She looked down at her flip-flops and said, "Yep. FDA approved! But, oops, somebody done stealed-the-toes right off of these steel-toed-shoes!"

They laughed, picked up the bag of vegetables, and Lourdes said, "Go ahead. I'll follow you."

Miguel walked in front of Lourdes, and turning around playfully asked, "How's my driving?"

On a sizzling Sunday, Eli, still in his long sleeves and suit, handed Lourdes a bulletin saying, "It will be hot and humid with a heat index of one hundred and five degrees. We are under a heat advisory."

Katie, also arriving at King's Community Church, leaned in and told Lourdes, "I bet next week he wears a short-sleeved shirt and a tie."

Everyone seemed to fade a little under the heat, although summer wouldn't officially begin until the third week of June.

Avy seemed to be fading under the heat the most. So much so that Jesse made her promise to call and move her check-up appointment to next week.

She kept her promise and made an appointment for the same day Lourdes had her next check-up, June eleventh. Lourdes's due date was now nine long weeks away.

On June eleventh, Lourdes finished her appointment then drove back to the hospital to pick up Avy Faye, she found Avy sitting in the hallway.

When Avy spotted Lourdes, she smiled, and said, "They drew blood and took a chest x-ray. I think they'll be out in a minute. Do you want to wait here with me, or do you have someplace to go?"

"Nope, no place but here!" Lourdes tried to find a comfortable place on the hard, wooden bench, thinking the bench hadn't seemed so hard and uncomfortable before.

Avy was right, it was just a moment before she was called to go to the lab on the second floor.

Lourdes and Avy walked into a small x-ray reading lab where a young doctor said, "I can't let you go home today." He pointed to a spot on the x-ray. "You have some fluid on your lungs we need to drain off. After we do that, I think you'll have more energy."

Unflustered, Avy said, "Oh. Okay. I'll call Jesse to come here after work." Turning to Lourdes she asked, "Can you please take the kids home? I'll see if Big Momma can stay with them until Jesse gets there?"

"Oh sure, but can I get you anything? You don't have an overnight bag or anything."

"No, I'm fine. Really. I'll go home tomorrow, right?" Avy asked the doctor.

He nodded with a smile, saying, "Should."

Avy Faye was calm, but Lourdes didn't feel that way. Driving home alone was the strangest ride ever for Lourdes. The green trees and familiar scenery were unnoticed, replaced by the feeling she was abandoning Avy to a cold hospital with no one there to care for her.

Lourdes called Miguel and told him what was happening and asked if she should stay overnight with the kids. He suggested she should do whatever made Avy feel better - and taking care of the kids was probably what she wanted.

At Safehaven, Katie opened the door and told Lourdes that Jesse had already called. Jesse had also talked to Big Momma who was going to spend the night with the kids, he wouldn't leave Avy Faye's side.

The kids seemed okay and enjoyed a pancake supper with Katie before Lourdes drove them home.

They drained the fluid off of Avy's lungs, she was released the next day saying that she did feel more energetic. She told Lourdes she hadn't realized how tired she was feeling because it sort of crept up on her, and having less gunk in her lungs was a real boost. She would need to go back to the doctor the next week, and Jesse said he would make sure he was off to take her – promising to drive carefully.

The news the next week was good. Her lungs were still clear giving her so much more energy that she was able to take a stroll through *Target* with Jesse.

It was hot in Kingsville. It was particularly hot in the pink house. It was unbearably hot for a very pregnant Lourdes.

"I think all these fans do is take the hot air and move it around so it hits me with more force," Lourdes told Miguel. There were two fans directed at Lourdes as she sat sprawled on the couch with her legs apart so one fan could blow up her maternity dress.

The long awaited television set had been purchased and set up with a DVD player in the living room. Only a few channels came through the antenna, but the Memphis library had a good supply of DVD's to keep Lourdes entertained. But no amount of entertainment could take Lourdes's mind off the miserable heat.

Her seating position was unladylike, but she didn't care. "Ughhhhhh," was all she could say as she drank ice water.

Miguel brought her fresh water, along with a cool rag, before leaving to run an errand for Mr. Dallas.

After a couple of hours, Lourdes heard the familiar, happy rumbling of the old truck's engine. The sound had become a song to her.

Outside the door, Lourdes could hear Miguel talking to someone. She sat upright, thinking her current sitting position would not only embarrass her but anyone unfortunate enough to walk inside.

Mr. Dallas was first through the door then Miguel, who was carrying a large box - a room air conditioner.

"It is much too hot for you to be enduring this weather without the good air that God intended for us to enjoy!" Mr. Dallas spoke with his continual chuckle and ended his sentence with his familiar, "Lordy, Lordy."

Lourdes gave Mr. Dallas a hug, Miguel shook hands with him as Mr. Dallas left.

"Every time I see him he has a smile, or a gift, or some sort of good news. How did you get this?" asked Lourdes.

"I've been saving up some extra money, and when Mr. Dallas asked about you, I told him how hot you are, well, he said he'd pay for half of this so we could get a good one - and here we are! Now where do you want to put it?" Miguel asked, looking for plugs by the windows in the living room.

He thought for a minute and said, "I think we should put it in the bedroom so you can sleep better. If you want, we can move the TV in there, too."

Miguel and Lourdes walked into the bedroom to see if there was a suitable plug by a window.

"Wow! I can't believe it!" Lourdes felt like she had won the lottery with a winning ticket she didn't know she bought.

A mere thirty minutes later, Miguel had the air conditioner braced and running. The most luscious, satisfying air was blowing over Lourdes, who sat in the old wooden rocking chair Miguel had found.

Miguel carried the TV into the bedroom where they began to rearrange furniture with the baby in mind. Most of the limited furnishing in the pink house was now in the bedroom.

"Okay," Miguel said, "I think this is the best place for the TV now, but after the baby comes you might want to move it back to the living room so you can watch it while the baby sleeps. Or, if you're like my sisters, you'll want to sleep when the baby does because you won't be sleeping at night."

"Uh, Miguel . . . How long *are* you planning on staying here?" This was a conversation she'd had in her head many times but had never actually verbally broached the subject.

"I figured we'd stay for a little bit after the baby comes so you can have a chance to figure out what you want to do. You might want to keep the baby, or you might want my parents to raise the baby."

Lourdes knew from the speed Miguel answered he must have been having this conversation with his parents - but not with her.

Miguel continued, "You like your doctors here, and I like working for Mr. Dallas. Let's give it a while until you decide."

There was a pang of sorrow that blew over Lourdes along with the lovely, cool air. It would be hard to leave this place. The pink house, Avy Faye and the kids, Safehaven with Katie and Tucker, they were the closest thing to family she had ever known.

She knew she couldn't work for Mr. Dallas to keep the pink house. But if she gave up the baby - maybe she could find a place to work full-time and live nearby. That would let her keep the sense of belonging she found in Kingsville, which had escaped her for her entire life.

Give up the baby? Not see Miguel? If she went back to Texas and let his family raise the baby, then maybe she could still see Miguel.

Lourdes was deep in thought while the cool air blew over her.

Miguel smiled at her, the gentle creak of the rocking chair serenading a peaceful scene. Lourdes closed her eyes, hiding her invisible thoughts that were chasing a downward spiral.

Within the month, the news that had been good for Avy Faye took an abrupt turn. Katie spoke to Lourdes anxiously when she arrived at Safehaven. "You know Jesse took Avy to Memphis yesterday for another appointment."

Lourdes nodded her head. It was one of the few times that Lourdes hadn't driven her.

"Well . . . you know . . . it was not good . . . and they're not going to do anymore chemo." Every sentence fragment that came out of Katie's mouth was chopped with effort. "Several of us at church have decided to fast and pray for three days that the Lord will heal Avy Faye. I don't think you should fast because of the baby, but if you would like to join us in praying . . . well . . . I wanted to let you know."

The lump in Lourdes's throat wouldn't go away.

The kids came and played as they always did. Lourdes played with them and tended to their needs like she always did. She tried to keep the day normal. Maybe all wasn't lost, these fine and good people were going to go without eating to honor what the Bible taught them about prayer and fasting. And wasn't it true every time they were together it seemed Avy Faye would live and be just fine?

There was simply no way that Avy would actually die. Lourdes kept that thought and it comforted her.

Lourdes did pray with the others. For the first time ever, she stretched out her hopes and sent up her best shot in prayer.

Katie and Polly did not eat for three days. Lourdes kept wondering if one of them would faint from lack of food but no one fainted. Only Polly murmured a bit louder about the little everyday annoyances that an empty stomach would not let her ignore.

After the three-day fast, Jesse came to Safehaven to pick up the kids. Lourdes helped them gather their things, and when they left there was a sad smile on Katie's face. "Jesse said that Avy Faye told him it doesn't matter how much longer she lives, it matters to her how well she lives. She said that she has put herself into God's hands and that is the best place to be."

Lourdes nodded a hopeful nod.

The following day, Jesse brought the baskets of dirty clothes when he dropped off Angela and Eli at Safehaven. For whatever reason, there was more laundry than usual. He went to work, leaving Big Momma to stay with Avy.

That afternoon, Jesse picked up the children a little bit early; Lourdes went back to the pink house to do the baskets of laundry for Avy Faye.

Lourdes kept the laundry moving from the washer to the dryer, retreating to the coolness of their bedroom between loads. Miguel came home for dinner early. The heat was bearing down on the guys, too, which shortened their work day.

Tonight for dinner she had cooked Shepherd's Pie. Lourdes now considered her cooking as 'adequate.' Although not nearly as good a cook as Katie or Polly, she was greatly improved.

Around eight o'clock she finished Avy's laundry and decided to return it, since there were so many baskets, they might need something from them to wear the next day. Miguel offered to go with her, but Lourdes said Eli and Angela liked to help carry things, and that she would be right back.

Jesse wasn't home, or his car wasn't there anyway. Lourdes carried one of the baskets to the door and knocked. Big Momma's tiny frame was silhouetted in the doorway when she answered.

"It's bad. It's real bad," Big Momma whispered. She had a wide-eyed expression of concern that only intense love could evoke. "I told her to hang on, and that we'd get some medicine in her just as soon as Jesse gets back home."

From the front door Lourdes could see into the master bedroom. Avy was sitting with her feet hanging off the side of the bed, barely touching the floor. She was wearing the white nightgown Eli and Angela had given her for Mother's Day, which made a lovely contrast to her dark skin.

Her beautiful, bald head was tilted to one side and her look of bewilderment betrayed her thinking, which clearly said there was something happening inside of her body that she didn't understand. Avy, unaware someone was at the door, continued looking down with a strange expression, while Big Momma looked anxious.

"Ummm. I've got the laundry. Let me just bring it to the front door." Lourdes could see the kids playing a game while sitting on the living room floor. They had to have heard the door and knew Big Momma answered, but they didn't look up.

"Where is Jesse?" whispered Lourdes.

"Of all days, his work called and he had to run back to the office. Avy told him to go," answered Big Momma.

After four quick trips to her car to pick up the baskets of clean, folded laundry, Lourdes took a quick look at Avy and returned to Miguel's 1997 Honda Accord.

She started the engine, but didn't move. Looking at the dusty dashboard, she prayed, "Lord, we've prayed everything we know to pray - and done everything we know to do." That was all she said.

Backing out of the driveway, she returned to the pink house.

Within the hour, Avy died. Lourdes got the call from Katie where she learned Jesse had made it home in time. Eli and Angela were there to watch the EMT's put their mother into an ambulance.

The nurses at the emergency room commented how beautiful she looked - even in death.

Big Momma stayed with the kids until Katie and Tucker could pick them up and drive them to Memphis. Under the florescent light of the hospital hallway, Jesse would bend down on his knees, hold his children, and tell them their mother had gone to be with Jesus.

That night the little family all slept together in the same bed where just a few hours earlier Avy Faye had sat upon - not at all sure what was happening inside of her earthly body.

Lourdes and Miguel went over to the Blue household early the next day, not wanting to intrude - but eager to help, hoping that any small gesture would ease the pain of Jesse, Eli, and Angela.

The house was soon filled with hushed people.

The funeral would be in two days. And even though the medical community might have predicted the outcome of Avy's cancer, it came as a surprise to the rest of the world who knew and loved her. To them it only seemed right that God would heal her.

Eli and Angela wanted to go to Safehaven with Lourdes. Of course, Katie was only too happy to have them. They didn't want to talk about their mom. They didn't want to talk at all.

When the kids were outside playing in the garden, Lourdes, almost angrily, asked Katie, "She said that she put her life in God's hands *and then she died?*"

It was both a question and an angry statement.

Katie replied with a quivering lip, "I'm not happy about this either. I've only known her for a couple of years, but she was like a sister to me." Katie had to hold her right eye still as it had begun twitching again.

With a deep breath, Katie added, "The last thing that Avy would want now would be for me to turn my back on God - while she is running into His arms."

The town had a chill running through it even though the weather was steamy hot. It was mid-July. Lourdes had a quick realization that she didn't know what day it was and she hoped she didn't find out - she didn't want to re-live this experience once a year.

Katie said that Julie, Luke, and Caleb planned to drive down to attend the funeral. Ginny and Cracker Philpott would also be coming. Polly was planning a luncheon afterwards, which involved lots of phone calls and arranging. Everyone in town wanted to do something, so there would be plenty of volunteers to help with the set-up, cooking, and serving.

The funeral would be at eleven o'clock in the morning on Thursday, July sixteenth.

Miguel was asked to be a pall-bearer, along with Tucker and Luke. Jane's husband, Bob, would also be serving. Avy's two brothers were the other two.

Lourdes and Miguel drove to Safehaven to pick up Cracker and Ginny. Since parking would be a problem at little King's Community Church, people were car-pooling as much as possible.

Luke, Julie, and Caleb rode with Katie and Tucker. Baby Caleb was now twenty-one months old. Although he started walking later than most babies, when he did start, he started at a run. He was mostly just babbling but talking some.

Everyone was wearing dark colors, except for Caleb. No one was smiling, except for Caleb, oblivious to the pain all around him.

The church parking lot was full, so people were walking over from the parking lots across the street. All the residents of Kingsville had come to pay their respects.

Eli was outside, not making eye contact with anyone. He wandered a bit aimlessly, never straying far from the front door. Lourdes thought that he would have felt more comfortable if he had bulletins to pass out along with the weather report.

It was standing room only. A very pregnant Lourdes and an older Ginny were given a place at the front where the over-worked air conditioner seemed to have the ability to drop the temperature by at least a degree or two.

Hessie Hobbs veered left toward the piano and played one of Avy's favorite hymns, *Tis So Sweet to Trust in Jesus*.

Avy's family walked in to sit on the front row.   Jesse looked exhausted by grief.

Pastor Anderson stood up and began, "Avy Faye Baxter Blue leaves behind a beloved husband, Jesse, and her two beloved children, Eli and Angela . . . along with a host of family and friends.

This doesn't make sense. This isn't the ending that we hoped would happen. Her struggle is over, and we have to make sense of our grief and our life without the quiet joy that was Avy Faye.

The Bible tells us that 'to be absent from the body is to be present with the Lord.' Absent, in Greek, means to take a trip, to go abroad.

I remember the trip to Hawaii that Jesse and Avy took a few years ago. She described it as PARADISE! When they left, I wasn't at all sad to see them leave. I was happy for them to have the experience, and I knew we would be together again.

If they were to have told me they were moving to Hawaii and I would likely not see them for a long time - I'd be happy for them living in paradise but at the same time sad - I would miss their presence in my life.

If we went down to Madame Tussauds Wax Museum and had the perfect copy of Avy made then sat it in the same church pew every Sunday, well, we would still miss Avy. It's her essence - her spirit - her personality - how she blessed us - that's what we'll miss.

But imagine Avy in paradise right now. Imagine that someday we will all join her there. Imagine the beauty and the peace. Imagine the absence of fear and sickness. Imagine finally being joined with the creator of our souls."

Lourdes could feel Pastor Anderson's gaze turning toward her, causing her to squirm a bit.

"Imagine," he continued, "if you were trying to explain to a baby inside of its mother's womb about the world he or she would soon be entering. Would you talk about the taste of a perfectly cooked fillet, or homemade ice cream? Would you try to describe a perfect sunset?

It would be hard to convince a babe in the womb that there is color and freedom of movement, because all they know is a dark place with a constant whooshing sound.

Heaven for us is what the real world is for that baby: unfathomable, indescribable, but very real and very much to come.

Just because Avy isn't here today doesn't mean she isn't somewhere.

Avy left us all a gift. The very things she took with her on her trip are the very things that she left behind to anchor us to her. Faith. Hope. Love.

I Corinthians 13:13 says, 'These three things continue forever: faith, hope and love.'

Think of her love as a soft piece of yarn that you tie from your finger to hers. You're connected. Think of that yarn as infinitely long, travelling through space and time. You're still connected no matter how far apart you are. That is what is happening here. We are, and always will be, connected to Avy Faye by her faith and hope and love that will continue forever.

Take her love with you into your journey through life."

Jesse was nodding his head in agreement, even though he had a glazed expression.

Looking at Jesse, the pastor said, "The truth is that the depth of love we feel for someone is the equal measure of sorrow we will feel at their passing.

And oh, how we loved Avy Faye."

He paused for a moment, his face downcast.

"Now," Pastor Aaron said, "here is the question we have to answer for ourselves. Is there life – for us – after the passing of Avy Faye?"

Looking at Eli and Angela he said, "You have the best mom. She hasn't left you - not really. You may not see her for a while - but when you do she will want to hear all the adventures and fun stories you have to tell her."

Looking back at the melancholy crowd, Pastor Aaron Anderson felt the same heartbreak they were experiencing. Avy Faye was his friend, too. His famous broad grin failed him today. He ended with a prayer of gratitude for Avy's life.

The congregation left King's Community Church and stood, silently, outside in the heat, while the casket with the body of Avy Faye was placed into the hearse to be taken to Kingsville Cemetery.

It was Jesse's wish this phase would be a private event with the immediate family only. Eli and Angela would not be making this trip with their mom. Tucker drove them home with Big Momma.

Polly had done her job, and everyone filed back into the fellowship hall to eat and comfort each other. The ladies from town that attended the other churches across Deacon Street had come over to cook and serve to show their love and respect.

Baby Caleb needed to go home for his nap. Lourdes was weary and hot - ready to sit someplace cool - away from people. Julie drove them all back to Safehaven with Lourdes riding along in the front seat. Katie with Caleb, in his car seat, buckled in the back seat.

Caleb cooed something that sounded like, "Ohhhh . . . Shoot," only it wasn't, "shoot," it was the full-on bad word. His baby voice sang the profanity from high to low as though the word was gently, smoothly, gliding down a playground slide.

He said it several times. Julie sheepishly said, "Caleb, baby, say, 'Ohhhhh *silly*."

She quickly added, "I don't know where he got that from. Luke promises it wasn't him. We think he is trying to say something else, but we don't know what."

Caleb responded by melodically repeating the word that made his mother wince.

Katie, her right eye twitching, held his small fingers and breathed, "My sentiments exactly."

PIPER COMES

"**D**ue dates are good-for-*noth-thing*!" It was August sixteenth, and the highly anticipated birthing day had come and gone with no significant progress. "We worked so hard to get here and now . . . *nothing*!" an exasperated, uncomfortable Lourdes almost yelled at Miguel.

Lourdes's dreams, which had become wilder as the day approached, were the only interesting things happening for the residents of the pink house.

"Last night I dreamed I saw Jesse, he looked so sad and wouldn't talk to me, so finally I started singing, 'Have a beer . . . and some sympathy,'" she warbled with a twang. "Is that a real song? I don't think I've ever heard it before."

"I don't think so," Miguel laughed. "But it should be a country western song. Somebody totally needs to write that!"

Lourdes appreciated Miguel's curiosity in her morning dream report. One of her favorite, of the many, things she liked about him was how deeply amused he seemed at her crazy misadventures. She'd never felt uninhibited around anyone before, but Miguel let her be herself – and actually seemed to enjoy her company.

He never said so. Lourdes just liked to believe it was true.

In the month following Avy's death, the heat and thick humidity caused the clouds to drop fat beads of sweat down from the sky, as creation itself seemed to suffer from the heat.

Lourdes heard Eli would be back at church the next Sunday to hand out bulletins and warn folks about the heat advisory. That would be a good thing, as King's Community Church needed Eli as much as Eli needed King's Community Church.

Not wanting to admit her double sense of loss, Lourdes hid her feelings about her job passing away with Avy Faye. Angela and Eli would both be starting school next week, and Big Momma would be handling their after-school care.

Lourdes had lost her extra income along with her friend.

Sitting on a squishy couch at Safehaven, Jesse told Lourdes and Katie how he had to get through his day one minute at a time. When he started back to work, he would walk past parked cars in the parking lot and think, 'I just need to walk past those next few cars.' Then he would think, 'I just need to get past the tree at the end of the lot.' Then it was getting to the front door. Step-by-step his day crept by.

It was awful. He moaned while describing how he thought his heart would beat to the point of literally breaking. He feared something happening to Eli or Angela, daily combating those thoughts.

Lourdes dropped her gaze so Jesse wouldn't see her tears drop down onto the floor where she stood. She watched the drops fall, making a solemn thud when they splashed.

He told them he remembered nodding his head in agreement at the funeral that he would get through this, but now he knew he only nodded out of shock and habit. He wasn't at all sure he could get through this.

Katie said nothing to Jesse, she only rubbed and patted his hand, smiling feebly.

There was one lingering mystery from the day of the funeral. The American flag, which always flew outside of Safehaven, had been lowered to half-staff during the funeral. Everyone in town was at the funeral, leaving no good suspects as to who had done this touching act. Respectfully, they left it that way for a week.

Out of habit, and a desperate desire to help, Lourdes still played with Eli and Angela when the need arose. Everyone was trying to pretend things were normal. No one was fooled. Nothing was normal.

Going to the clinic once a week for her check-ups had become upsetting for Lourdes. Now travelling alone, every moment of the trip reminded her of driving Miss Avy.

After Miguel realized how this was affecting Lourdes, he arranged to take off so he could drive her to the appointments. Mr. Dallas was, of course, more than willing to accommodate his schedule.

It was almost time for Miguel to come home from work and Lourdes, who didn't much feel like standing in a hot kitchen cooking, decided spaghetti would be a quick fix.

Although the Mercantile was right across the street, and did have a nice variety of products, Lourdes didn't like going there because Clayton Hobbs was so unfriendly. However, once or twice a week she found herself shopping there, because as diligent as she tried to be with a shopping list she'd often find herself needing something.

Today she realized she needed spaghetti noodles.

Walking in, he acknowledged her with his typical, "Humph."

Lourdes quickly found the pasta and took it to the register to pay.

Without looking at Lourdes, Clayton gruffly said, "I just heard on the news about a girl who went into the hospital to have a baby and she came out with no arms or legs."

This had to have been the most disturbing and frightening thing anyone could have said to a soon-to-give-birth Lourdes.

Speechless, she stared at him in shock.

He gave her change for her five dollar bill and continued, "Just you think about that."

It wasn't from the humidity, but tears fell down her face like sweat on her short walk home.

Soon as Miguel was home, Lourdes, weepy, told him what Clayton had said.

"Ignore him. That's not going to happen to you. I can't believe anyone would talk to a pregnant girl like that!"

But nothing Miguel said really calmed her nerves, and he seemed to know it.

He told her about all his cousins and sisters and friends who had babies with no complications. Lourdes felt she heard a hint of reservation in his voice, as though he couldn't promise her good health.

A few days passed before Lourdes was able to stop obsessing about Mr. Hobbs's remark. Although she couldn't fully put it out of her mind, the fact that he ended his tale of fear with, "just you think about that," made her adamant that she NOT think about it - ever again.

The women of King's Community Church did not have a formal baby shower for Lourdes like they would have if Avy hadn't just died. A celebratory get-together would have been a sore reminder of who wasn't there. Instead, they gathered up gifts of crib sheets, blankets, clothes, diapers, and typical baby items.

Polly bought them a crib and mattress. Julie sent them a huge package of useful baby items that Caleb had outgrown.

Together Lourdes and Miguel fashioned a corner for the baby in their bedroom.

Lourdes was now a week past her due date. The girls at the clinic assured her she and the baby were just fine, but they couldn't do anything about how miserable and enlarged she felt in the Tennessee heat.

School would be starting tomorrow, the twenty-first of August. Angela told Lourdes she was excited to go to Kindergarten. Even Eli seemed ready to start third grade.

With Katie and Tucker going into Memphis to buy supplies for the bed and breakfast, Polly and Lourdes were both at Safehaven to play with the kids on this last day of summer vacation.

Angela was lazily sitting on Polly's lap while Eli watched TV.

Without making eye contact with anyone Eli said, "Mama died wearing the nightgown we gave her for Mother's Day." His voice was hushed, and it seemed to Lourdes that she heard Avy's quiet tone.

Polly, unusually gentle, answered, "Darlin', wasn't that the best present, ever? The thing that was touching her skin as she went from this world to the next was your gown. Why, it was like you were giving her a hug, and she could feel your touch."

Angela, who must have been listening, chirped, "Me, too!"

"That's right, sweetie, and you, too!" Polly answered with a loving squeeze.

Apparently, this was something that had been bothering both of the children and this new way of thinking brought a measure of peace.

Angela hopped off of Polly's lap to sit beside Eli.

Lourdes, a bit in awe, whispered, "That was so wise!! How did you ever think to say that so quickly, right off the top of your head?"

"Sometimes I even amaze myself at the smart things I say! But most of the time, I can't even remember where I left my car keys. And once I find them, I have to remember where I wanted to go," Polly chuckled.

"Why just last week," Polly continued, "I went to the mall and kept having that nagging feeling that I'd forgotten something, so I looked down just to make sure I remembered to put on my pants!"

Lourdes laughed a much needed giggle.

Just a few minutes later, Angela asked if she could go get Katie's craft basket. Lourdes lumbered off the couch to go with her.

It wasn't long before Lourdes and Angela returned with the basket. Angela asked, "Miss Polly, can you help me tie this ribbon around my finger so I can remember I'm still tied to Mom?"

Lourdes saw a painful smile shoot across Polly's face. "Of course, baby. Should we make a ring for your finger or a bracelet?"

Eli wanted one, too. Both Eli and Angela decided they wanted blue bracelets made of thin, curling ribbon.

The next day school started for the children. Later, Jesse told Katie and Lourdes how he gathered them, dressed in their finest new school clothes, and drove them to Crocket Elementary School, where they both went happily into their new classrooms, wearing the blue ribbon bracelets.

The following day was another check-up day for Lourdes. There was a chance of rain and because of the extreme heat, the rainstorms could turn severe.

Lourdes still hated going for her appointments because of people poking around her private area, especially if there wasn't any good news about her progress.

At three in the afternoon her routine visit brought unexpected results. Lourdes was developing preeclampsia, which required a quick delivery. Miguel drove Lourdes straight to the hospital - the same hospital where Lourdes and Avy had eaten so many cups of Jell-O.

Miguel called Katie and then called his parents. Lourdes didn't want to call Aunt Connie until after the baby was born. She especially didn't want to talk about her future plans because Lourdes didn't have any idea what was about to happen.

Lourdes was given an I.V. drip with medication to start her labor contractions. The cramping started pretty quickly, paralleling how quickly she began to panic.

The birthing room was large, dark, and had the ambiance of a cheap motel, much like the *Motel 6* she and Miguel stayed at after the wedding.

The doctors had explained the mechanics of giving birth, but it felt very different lying here, wearing a white hospital gown with several monitors hooked up and beeping.

In a forceful whisper Lourdes said to Miguel, "Do you know how they measure if I'm dilating? WITH THEIR FINGERS! I thought at least in the hospital they would use a ruler or something. I don't want someone constantly in my . . . down in my . . . area!"

Miguel excused himself when she was being examined. Lourdes and Miguel had always been very polite and proper toward each other. They had politely not passed gas in front of each other. Now, there were all kinds of sounds emitting from Lourdes, and this gown left nothing to the imagination.

Other than when she was being examined, Lourdes didn't want Miguel more than two feet away from her. Unable to leave her side, Miguel was feeling hungry.

The progress was slow and limited. Lourdes now had an epidural, which was making her drowsy and nod off occasionally.

Lourdes seemed to be napping, and Miguel thought this was a good time to go to the cafeteria or at least a vending machine. Walking down the hall he found Katie, Tucker, and Mr. Dallas standing in a waiting area.

"Hey!" Miguel stopped, happy to feel like he had some family support there.

"How is Lourdes?" asked Katie, who had cracker crumbs spattered across the front of her shirt.

"She's okay. Nervous. Kind of sleepy from the medicine," he shrugged.

Katie looked down at the mess on her shirt and started to wipe the crumbs off. "Tucker, why didn't you tell me how I looked! I came over here and I started feeling antsy, so I started munching on crackers." The crumbs had not only drizzled down her shirt but all over the floor.

"I'm on my way to the cafeteria. Lourdes doesn't want me to leave her, but she was asleep. I figured I wouldn't be gone just a minute. Do you mind going to check on her?"

"I'd love to!" Katie practically trotted to the Nurses Station where was told to go to Room 3.

Awakened by Katie coming into the room, Lourdes tearfully moaned, "It hurts."

"I'm sorry, sweetheart," Katie said as she stroked Lourdes's head.

Lourdes said, "I'd rather just go home. Do you think they'd let me have the baby there?"

"Well, if you wait and have the baby here, then you can all go home together," Katie sweetly answered.

"I just really want the pain to stop," Lourdes said, eyes closed, half-asleep.

"Are you in a lot of pain?"

"Sometimes," Lourdes answered, sounding mournful.

Luckily, Katie knew about epidurals from when Julie had Caleb and excused herself to go ask the nurse for help. The nurse called Dr. Mason, Lourdes's favorite doctor from the clinic, who came right away to check on Lourdes. Sure enough, she called the anesthesiologist, who was able to adjust the epidural, giving Lourdes some relief.

Katie and Tucker went home with the promise from Miguel to call the minute something happened.

Lourdes drifted off into a semi-dreamlike state; she dreamed she had the baby, but it turned into creamy-colored goo. The goo was going down the bathroom sink drain and as she tried to scoop it out with her hands, it simply ran through her fingers down the drain.

Afraid Miguel would be mad at her for turning the baby into goo, she woke up. When she told him, he laughed, held her hand, and reminded her it was a bad dream because she was stressed.

It was a long night for Lourdes and Miguel. There were no secrets left to Miguel about Lourdes's body. There was nothing romantic about its display.

The nurses and doctors were attentive and kind.

On August twenty-third at six in the morning, an eight pound, two ounce baby girl was born.

Miguel had just seen the majestic atrocity called birth. He stood beside Lourdes's bed, stroking her hair, looking with extraordinary fondness at the two girls.

"Well, what's her name?" was the first question out of Katie's mouth when she popped her head in the door.

Miguel answered, "Piper Faye Rico."

"Piper. That's really pretty," beamed Katie.

Lourdes looked at Miguel and said, "He really likes airplanes and I saw the magazine that Avy gave him . . . he'd been looking through it . . . and I saw an ad for a Piper airplane. I thought how that would be the perfect name for her, Piper."

Lourdes and Miguel looked into each other's red, bleary, tired eyes and smiled.

Katie peeked at Piper, who was wrapped up in a hospital blanket, and quietly said to the baby, "So this is what you look like, pretty girl."

Piper had plenty of thick black hair. A healthy-sized baby, she had full cheeks. Her dark eyes were open as she tried to take in her new world.

The hospital room had no flowers or teddy bears sent by loving grandparents. Since Lourdes and Piper were doing fine, and because Lourdes didn't have health insurance, they would have twenty-four hours until time to check out.

At noon the next day, Miguel and Lourdes put Piper into the same Honda that had driven them to Tennessee, buckled her into the car seat that Jane had loaned them, and drove Piper Faye Rico home to the pink house.

Their first visitors were Jesse, Eli and Angela Blue. Eli and Angela sat politely on the floor in the overly-warm living room while their dad handed the new parents a gift box with a baby blanket inside.

Both children had replaced the blue ribbon bracelets that connected them to their mom with ones made of braided yarn, which was long enough for their fingers to fiddle and twirl between.

"Hey, guys, do you know what they named the baby?" Jesse asked them.

"Piper?" answered Angela with an unsure voice.

"Piper Faye," said Lourdes.

"Faye! My mom's second name is Faye, too!" Angela said excitedly.

"Yes, I know. I picked that name because of your mom," smiled Lourdes.

Eli looked at the baby, then turning his attention to more important matters said, "There is a hurricane in the Gulf of Mexico. They don't know where it's going to track just yet. They just draw wide lines showing where it might go, and when it gets closer to shore then they draw the lines closer together. It's called 'The Cone of Uncertainty.'"

Such a large weather event for Eli was equivalent to the excitement of the birth of a child.

Jesse, Eli, and Angela hugged the new family and went home, leaving the brand new baby with her brand new parents.

That night was awful. The baby cried and cried. Unprepared, Lourdes and Miguel were both exhausted and exasperated. It crossed Lourdes's mind that taking Piper to Miguel's parents might be the best idea.

The next day, Katie dropped by the pink house when Miguel was at work. Lourdes, miserable, sitting in a heap of tears, said, "We tried everything. We even tried to put this bouncer thing together in the middle of the night, and Miguel was looking for batteries so we could put her in that, but *nothing worked!*" She pointed at the bouncer as if were wicked and unwilling to do its job.

Lourdes wailed, "I feel like I'm living in the 'Cone of Uncertainty' like Eli was talking about. I don't know what I'm doing. I don't know where I'm going!" Lourdes was already seated when she said that, and if it were possible, slumped even farther into the couch.

"I need my mother to help me - ***and I don't have one***!" Lourdes sobbed, her hands covering her face.

Katie understood the blunt truth of Lourdes's situation. Lourdes had spoken so forcefully, Katie could almost see the raging, gaping wound in Lourdes' heart.

Shaken, she put her hand on Lourdes's shoulder and compassionately said, "I'm certain God has a good plan for you," Katie spoke kindly. "Tell you what we'll do. Tonight, you and Miguel bring the baby - and whatever else you need - to my house, and I'll help you with the night shift. Maybe you can get a little sleep and things will look brighter."

Without question, Lourdes accepted the offer. She wasn't convinced God would help but she knew Katie would.

They accepted that offer for the next three days and nights. It took several adults to take care of one tiny baby.

Over the weekend, Safehaven Bed and Breakfast would be having paying guests, the fussy newborn and her parents would have to go home to the pink house. But they would arrive in better spirits and with a little more training on the care and feeding of babies from the skilled, loving hands of the folks at Safehaven.

Before they went back to the pink house, Mr. Dallas dropped by to meet the baby. Piper was, as she had been, fussy. "Give that baby something to eat," Mr. Dallas said, looking at Piper. "She needs a chicken leg or a cheeseburger. Cheeseburger . . . double cheese - American and Provolone." He continued to chuckle and repeat, "Provolone."

They all walked outside, and while Miguel hooked the car seat into the base, Katie said to Lourdes, "If she gets fussy and you feel overwhelmed, put her into the stroller that Hessie gave you and just walk around - even if it is just inside the house."

That advice came in handy a couple of days later when a tired, frustrated Lourdes felt like lashing out at the uncooperative baby.

No amount of rocking or patting or shushing would calm Piper. She wasn't hungry, and her diaper was dry.

"Why don't you just shut-up!" Lourdes's exhausted voice was dripping with choked fury.

She thought about fashioning an advertisement: FREE TO GOOD HOME – EIGHT DAY OLD BABY.

"No," she mumbled to herself, "Miguel would get mad."

Hot tears streamed down her face. Quivering, she put Piper into the stroller and took several steps back to lessen the sounds of crying assaulting her ears. She thought for a moment that she actually hated this child.

One minute later, Piper stopped crying, opened her eyes and looked around. Lourdes felt the most miserable remorse she had ever felt. How could she hate this baby?

She knew she didn't hate Piper. She crumpled onto the floor, her face crossed with lines of pain. Failure as a person - failure as a mother, she wondered what else was she going to be the world's worst at being?

After a few deep breaths, Lourdes stood up, stoically saying aloud, "Okay," and tended to her baby.

The rest of the day was better. When she told Miguel what happened, he told her babies aren't easy and not to be so hard on herself.

When Katie came over the next day, they sat in the bedroom where it was cool. Lourdes told her about her meltdown and asked, "What's wrong with me?"

Katie, with her usual deliberation said, "Motherhood isn't a fairy tale. Piper is learning how to be a person at the same time you're learning how to care for a newborn person.

And those two things are colliding while your body is trying to adjust to not being pregnant anymore, and you're doing all of that with limited sleep."

Katie took Piper from Lourdes's arms and cooed to the baby, "Hey, you . . . be sweet to your momma . . . she's gonna be your best friend."

Lourdes smiled while Katie rocked the baby. Maybe it was Katie's calm voice, maybe it was because Piper was quiet, maybe she felt a fleeting moment of happiness, whatever happened, it was the first glimmer of hope that Lourdes felt since the baby was born. Piper really was a cute baby – when someone else was holding her.

Gently rocking and patting the baby, Katie spoke softly as she said, "You know Miguel's parents called and reserved a room for next weekend."

"Yes, I know they're coming," Lourdes said uneasily. "And they've been talking to Miguel about raising the baby."

Katie swallowed, "Well, this is a hard situation for you. Letting someone else adopt the baby isn't abandoning the baby. Sometimes the absolute essence of caring for a baby is to let it be in a place where it can thrive.

I just worry that you'll make a decision when you're tired and sleep-deprived and not able to think clearly."

"I know," answered Lourdes. "I just thought Piper would be like the Mother Theresa of babies or something."

Amused, Katie said, "I doubt even Mother Theresa was," holding up her hands gingerly to make air quotes, "'Mother Theresa' when she was a baby."

The next weekend was Labor Day weekend. Miguel's parents came. His dad, Samuel Rico, was a solid man. You could tell he had enjoyed the food from his mobile restaurant for decades. Delores Rico was smaller, but still stout. Both were dressed in their Sunday finest, he wore a gray suit with a blue tie, she wore a colorful, flower-printed dress with a thin blue belt. They had pleasant expressions and kind words when they met Lourdes for the first time.

Lourdes wanted to present the baby as well as she could to Piper's grandparents. Wearing a pink, checked outfit with plenty of lace and flowers, Piper was placed in the arms of her grandmother.

Samuel and Delores Rico couldn't take their eyes off of Piper. They cuddled and cooed to the point that Lourdes realized they couldn't have cared if she were there or not. A hormonal Lourdes didn't like feeling ignored.

Lourdes's opinion of Roy Rico, their favored son, had slid to an all-time low. Roy was popular and loved – everything Lourdes had thought any girl would want. Turned out, he wasn't wonderful. The only wonderful thing about him was that he had a very nice, kind brother.

Miguel's parents weren't paying too much attention to him either, but Miguel must have been used to this as it didn't seem to bother him in the least.

Lourdes could tell he was glad to see them and proud to show them this beautiful baby, who was behaving surprisingly well.

It seemed like Lourdes would have appreciated the extra help they gave while they were visiting. They were more than willing to help take care of Lourdes and the baby. They would stand in the hot kitchen cooking - dishes or clothes need only have a speck of something on it before they were washed and put away. However, Lourdes rather resented it. She had a smoldering suspicion they were going to try and convince her to let them take the baby. And if it was a package deal, they would take Lourdes, too - if they had to.

Katie told Lourdes she had a different impression of them. While they were at Safehaven they were mannered, friendly, and personable.

Samuel and Delores Rico returned to Texas the Tuesday after Labor Day, without taking any of Lourdes's family members with them.

They left behind several meals in the freezer so Lourdes would only have to defrost a delicious dinner. They also left behind a baby gift that turned out to be the most wonderful thing Lourdes received – a baby swing that rocked from side-to-side. The calming affect it had on Piper was indescribable, it was like meditation for a newborn.

The baby swing, Lourdes's calming hormones, and learning the rhythm of having a newborn in the house were all having a positive effect on the residents of the pink house.

By the end of September, Piper was starting to sleep a few extra hours at night. It wasn't all night, but enough of a stretch that it helped Lourdes and Miguel. Life was getting better.

The beginning of October brought cooler air and cooler heads, with the added bonus of Angela's birthday. Jesse put on the best princess party that he could with the help of party-planning Polly.

It was one more holiday in a long line of holidays that they would have to venture through without Avy.

Aunt Connie had now been told the whole story, everything about Roy and Miguel, about Las Vegas, about Kingsville, and about Piper.

Lourdes was right to think Aunt Connie wouldn't have wanted her to come home with a baby. She congratulated Lourdes, wished her well, and ended the phone call rather quickly. Lourdes assumed, probably rightly, the call was short so she wouldn't have opportunity to ask for anything from Aunt Connie.

It was over dinner, the conversation Lourdes had been dreading since they arrived at the pink house popped out of Miguel's mouth.

Miguel had made the decision that he was ready to settle on a moving date. Maybe he missed his old job and wanted a career with his family instead of being a helping hand to Mr. Dallas. Maybe seeing his parents made him realize he wanted to go home. Maybe he didn't like the nighttime hours required to care for a newborn. Maybe he just wanted to wake up in Texas - he didn't explain. He had simply decided this current living arrangement would end by Christmas.

Lourdes nodded, taking the news quietly, even graciously, without betraying her soul-crushing anguish. Miguel had earned her respect, and she wouldn't sully the moment, or this experience, with her own neediness. She would either have to find a way to provide for herself and Piper, or the baby would need to be raised by someone else.

MARCELA

The name, Marcela, had been entering Miguel's conversations like the dripping of a leaky faucet - slowly and annoyingly. Within a couple of weeks, it was like the constant gush of a rusty, burst pipe.

Marcela worked in Memphis at a tractor supply company where Miguel often went to buy things for Mr. Dallas. Marcela was pretty, bordering on exotic looking. Marcela had jet black hair and features he thought made her look like a gypsy. Marcela had a favorite club where she liked to go dancing. Marcela was attending community college to get her associates degree. Marcela drove a shiny, new red truck. Marcela didn't like diet drinks. Marcela sent him a picture of a sink hole that had opened up in front of a fast-food restaurant.

Lourdes felt harassed by the name Marcela.

Even so, the cool, crisp, mid-October day invigorated the steps of Katie and Lourdes, who was carrying Piper, down the driveway to the mailbox at Safehaven. The canopy from the Tennessee trees beautifully signaled the changing season. Looking up at them

Lourdes said, "Miguel and I were talking about Angela's birthday party and how hard it was for everyone. I didn't know it before, but Miguel let it slip that his birthday is coming up on November third. Do you think we could do a party for him?"

"We ABSOLUTELY should do something for him!" The lilt in Katie's voice always brought a lighthearted fun into the conversation. "Our church always does something around Halloween - we call it the Fall Festival. I'm not sure what day it's scheduled for though. Do you know what day the third falls on?"

"I don't off the top of my head," Lourdes answered, poking the pacifier back into Piper's mouth.

Retrieving the assortment of bills, magazines and flyers from the mailbox, they lazily strolled back to Safehaven. Settling a sleepy Piper into her bouncer, Lourdes had a quiet moment with Katie, so she said, "Miguel met a girl, Marcela, and I think he likes her."

Lourdes didn't make eye contact with Katie when she said it, preferring to watch her drowsy child.

"Really?" Katie asked with a surprised tone. "You know, I always forget that you two aren't a couple in the traditional sense of the word. Why do you think so? How do you feel about it?"

"Well, I mean . . . he has every right to do what he wants to do. And . . . well, I mean, we agreed that we would do this until the end of the year by Christmas. And then I'd have to decide what I want to do next. That was the agreement," Lourdes's voice trailed off.

Katie's voice continued in a softened tone, "It doesn't seem fair or easy that you should have to be making such life-changing decisions when your baby is so small.

I remember right after I had Julie, I couldn't decide what clothes I should wear for the day. Small decisions seemed overwhelming because my brain was filled with trying to figure out what I was doing."

Sipping on a cup of tea, Katie continued, "But on the other hand, I applaud Miguel for taking such good care of you and Piper and, really, all of us. You've both been such a blessing over these past months. I don't know how we would have made it without you two."

When Lourdes did look up, Katie's blue eyes locked onto Lourdes's brown ones. After a few moments, Katie patted Lourdes's leg, "We'll try to help you figure something out."

"I know for sure I can't go back to my aunt's house. I called her, and, well . . . anyway," Lourdes said, not finishing her sentence with a shrug of her shoulders.

Katie patted Lourdes's leg again. Lourdes wasn't so sure Katie could help this time, but it was comforting to have someone care. Fighting the welling tears, she murmured, "Thank you."

Waiting until her voice strengthened, Lourdes said, "I know that living in the pink house is a perk for Miguel from Mr. Dallas, and I can't stay there. Do you know of any other house or place that I could stay? Or a job where I could work? I mean, I'd really like to stay around Kingsville, I mean, I've never before felt so much like I belonged . . ." A very large lump clogged her throat.

Until Kingsville, Lourdes had never felt wanted in her entire life. She didn't know who her father was - her mom was ensnared to addictions, so when she disappeared no one knew if she was the victim of foul play or had simply decided to live somewhere else. Her disappearance did leave Aunt Connie with a child to raise. Connie, just like Miguel, did the right thing.

The consequence of mandatory care left Lourdes feeling like no one would voluntarily choose her.

Deciding to be honest, Lourdes choked out the words, "I feel like I'm not worth anything." Her raspy voice said the simple sentence, which contained a lifetime of self-analysis.

"Sweetheart, that's just not true," Katie furrowed her brows. "You may believe that about yourself that, but it isn't true.

You have a good heart and a sweet spirit. Even if those good qualities were formed out of painful experiences - you're so caring.

I've seen you with Avy and Eli and Angela. Their lives were better when you joined their journey."

Katie didn't say anything for a minute. The memory of Avy Faye filled the air. Firmly, Katie continued, "One day you will overcome all of these terrible obstacles, and you'll see that you like who you've become . . . and you'll know that God loves you . . . and that will be enough. Because every person – with plenty of friends and a great family background or not – has to discover that the relationship that matters most is the one between themselves and God."

Lourdes looked up. Katie's gaze was intense. The room was quiet. Out the window, Lourdes could see golden leaves gently blowing in the peaceful setting of Safehaven.

Unwavering, Katie firmly said, "**God is more than enough**. Once you have that settled in your soul, you've found freedom. For me, that's when I began to truly enjoy my life."

Lourdes barely absorbed what Katie said - only wishing it were true.

There was a knock at the door, and Polly peeped inside. "Hey, y'all, I want you to see what Peter bought me as a surprise! Come on out here!"

Lourdes thought most people would have sensed they were intruding on something - but not Polly. With an enthusiastic wave, she said, "Come on! Come on!"

Katie smiled at Lourdes and joined Polly, while Lourdes stood at the door not wanting to leave a sleeping Piper alone in the house.

Parked in front of Safehaven was a gleaming, solid black, convertible sports car.

Her voice sounding like smooth jazz, Katie said, "Snazzy!"

Polly, with child-like glee, looked greedily at her new car. "When you get to be my age, you should get a little sports car like this. It rejuvenates you! Except that it's hard to bend down and get in and out of the car. And my left ankle has a little arthritis, so sometimes the clutch is a little painful. But boy! I feel young!"

Polly danced a bit on her arthritic ankle, joyfully showing off her new toy.

"Polly," Katie said as they settled into the soft chairs back inside of Safehaven, "You know that Miguel and Lourdes are only supposed to stay until the end of the year, but Lourdes wants to stay with us here in Kingsville when Miguel goes home to Texas. So we need to brainstorm a way to find a house and a job for Lourdes. Do you have any ideas?

"But," Katie paused looking serious, "We don't know God's plan for your life, and it just may be that you aren't supposed to stay here."

Lourdes faintly nodded her head.

"Well," Polly jumped in, "I don't know if I KNOW a lot, or if I'm NOSY a lot, but I'll get right on it and try to find something for you! Did you ask Archie if you could stay in the pink house anyway? Nobody has lived there before you two for quite some time."

Lourdes shook her head. The thought hadn't occurred to her.

"Well, I'll start there. I've known Mr. Archibald Dallas for years, so I'll just see what I can do," her southern smile encouraged Lourdes.

A fussy Piper forced Lourdes to go home. Walking back to Lourdes's car, Katie quietly said, "Talk to Miguel."

Lourdes smiled and vaguely nodded, knowing she had no intention of talking to Miguel.

At the pink house, Lourdes lay Piper down in her crib. Sleepy Piper lay on her back with her tiny arms resting above her head. Piper closed her eyes, took a deep breath, and started moving her lower lip like she was gaining nutrition from the air, her lips stilled, and then she smiled. Soon her bottom lip continued the motion when Lourdes put a pacifier in her mouth.

Noticing, maybe for the first time, how fragile and perfect all her features were, Lourdes took Piper's hand, which immediately closed around her finger, and watched as the baby would stop sucking the pacifier to smile, only to resume the sucking motion.

"What? Are you having crazy dreams like your momma does?" Lourdes stroked the baby's hair while remembering the Valentine card that Angela had given her parents which said, '*You hold my heart in your hands.*' Whispering over Piper's small face said, "I'll take care of your heart. I promise."

Over dinner Miguel didn't have to bring up Marcela - Marcela called. Answering, cheerfully, he said, "Hey . . . Yeah . . . Well, I can't believe he would do that on purpose." Miguel laughed. "Right . . . See you tomorrow. Bye."

"Marcela?" asked Lourdes, barely able to mask the boiling undercurrent of whatever unnamed emotion she was feeling.

"Yeah," was all he said.

"Miguel, we need to talk about December. I know we agreed to stay with this arrangement until then. That's closing in - and now with Marcela - I think we need to figure out what we're going to do. I mean, have you even told Mr. Dallas yet?"

"OH LOOK! DID YOU SEE THAT?" Miguel was staring at Piper, who was resting in her bouncer on the table.

Alarmed, Lourdes asked, "What's wrong?"

"She just smiled. Have you seen her smile before?"

"Well, maybe, kind of. She makes the oddest expressions sometimes." Lourdes didn't want to tell Miguel about the sleepy smile she had seen earlier. It was a private moment between mother and daughter.

"Well, that was a smile! Did you see her dimple?" Miguel picked up Piper and in his best baby-voice said, "Yes, it was. Yes, it was. Sweet girl." He kissed her dimple and put her back in the bouncer.

"Lourdes," his voice now matter-of-fact, "I'm always going to be Piper's uncle, and . . ." his voice trailed off a tad, "and you and I are friends."

That seemed to be all of the conversation that either of them knew to say. They finished eating their dinner quietly with no happy dinnertime chatter.

The church Fall Festival would be held on Sunday night. Eli and Angela decided on their costumes, Angela found a tiara and faux pearls to set off a pink, princess dress. Eli wanted to be a weather event, so Jesse created a passable tornado by bending white poster board into a cone shape then wrapping it with swirling black yarn. Eli's head poked out the top.

All of the fine folks of Kingsville, Tennessee got together for one big celebration, alternating between the church parking lots. This year, St. Anthony's Catholic Church was the host.

Piper, dressed as an orange and black striped kitten, spent her first Halloween sleeping through most of the excitement, not at all interested in any of the festivities. Lourdes drew whiskers onto Piper's chubby cheeks, and her heavy costume turned out to be a little much for the warm evening.

Lourdes and Miguel pushed her stroller around the church parking lot where various games were set-up. Having met lots of the town's people, they enjoyed visiting their neighbors. Miguel even won a cake from a game of musical chairs. Lourdes thought the cake was worth a thousand dollars to him from the amount of pride and fun he had beating out ten other adults and children.

Miguel's birthday was just a few days away, which fell on a Thursday. The family at the pink house celebrated with pizza. Miguel's real party was planned for Saturday night at Safehaven. Katie suggested they play a game called Bunco, a dice game involving no skill, plenty of time for snacks, and several tables of players.

Megan, a girl from church, was hired to babysit all the kids whose parents would be playing.

Lourdes and Miguel were the first people to show up. Tucker and Katie, placing finishing touches on the snacks, were in the kitchen. Lourdes went with Megan to settle Piper for the evening.

"Hey, man, what's up?" Miguel asked as he shook Tucker's hand.

Tucker, holding a golf ball, said, "I'm not much of a golfer, but a friend of mine said that if you microwave a golf ball for a few seconds you can hit it farther."

After putting it in the microwave a few seconds, Tucker and Miguel walked the ball, which was making a crackling, popping sound, outside. Before they reached the door, the golf ball burst in a mini-explosion startling everyone in the house. Katie dropped to her knees as if it were a gunshot. Lourdes ran toward the sound.

"What in the world was that?" Katie howled as she stood up, looking around the room.

Tucker, whose right side of his face now had a thick black smudge, held up the ruined golf ball as he staggered up from the floor.

"Are you all right?" Miguel asked Tucker, while rubbing his own ringing ears.

Tucker nodded. After they all realized they were lucky not to have been seriously injured from pure stupidity, Tucker said, "Well, so much for my science lab experiment!"

"That's one way to get this party started . . . a bad way," quipped Katie.

The mood lightened considerably as the guests arrived.

There were enough guests to have three card tables set up to play Bunco. Katie started by explaining the simple rules to Lourdes and Miguel, Polly and Peter, Jane and Bob, Pastor Aaron and Mary Frances, Jesse, and Big Momma.

Jesse hadn't done anything social since Avy Faye passed away.

Polly made Miguel a moist Carrot Cake with homemade cream cheese frosting with caramelized pecans on top.

An easy fun permeated the room, while pockets of laughter would erupt around the card tables.

At nine o'clock the kids and adults were ready to go home.

Eli and Angela were saying their goodbyes to Katie and Tucker. Angela must have felt a little overcome with the feelings of playfulness and kept repeating, "Thank you for the wonderful things! Thank you for the WONDERFUL THINGS!"

It was just so adorable, the group sighed an audible, "Awwwww."

Jesse confided that he was glad he came, finding comfort in the cushy chairs of Safehaven, surrounded by friends whose love continued to wash off the rough edges of his grief.

Jane's three-year-old son must have felt left out of the conversation, saying to Tucker, "Hey! I kicked your cat!"

Laughter was unavoidable, so, in the end, he got his recognition and everyone left happy, except maybe the cat.

With the party over, Lourdes and Miguel took Piper home to the pink house. Lourdes kept a smile on her face, remembering the fun and tenderness of the evening. Miguel kept looking at his cell phone.

Lourdes realized he was checking for texts or missed calls. Her smile faded and her happiness diminished as Marcela crashed into their evening.

After settling Piper into her crib, Miguel walked outside where Lourdes could see him talking on the phone.

When he came back in the house, neither of them mentioned the phone call – as if he hadn't gone outside at all.

The next day they arrived at King's Community Church where Eli handed them the bulletin saying, "We should have moderate temperatures all week." There was a hint of disappointment in his voice that he didn't have anything more exciting to report. It seemed all of America was in for a week of boring weather.

Jesse had dropped Eli off at church while he stayed home with Angela, who wasn't feeling well. The next day, a doctor's appointment told them Angela had a virus. A viral infection takes a week to ten days to work through; and since no medications really help, it would be a pretty miserable week.

Jesse left his sick child with Katie, who sat the unhappy Angela on her lap. With a soft, maternal voice Katie said, "Tell me where it hurts."

"My virus hurts," moaned Angela.

Lourdes dropped by to return a pan, which previously was filled with leftovers; but not wanting Piper around a sick child, she left it quickly. Walking back to her car, she realized she needed to get used to taking care of the baby without much help. This would be good practice for her life to come.

Miguel had been more than just a lot of help with Piper - he doted on her. He came home from work, washed his hands, picked up the baby and held her until dinnertime, then after giving the baby her bath, he helped clean up the kitchen.

Piper's sleeping had stretched into a six or seven hours during the night. The nice little routine felt heavenly to Lourdes.

The week went by quickly, but by the end of the week Miguel began to act a little strangely. After the dinner was finished on Thursday night, with Piper dreaming in her crib, he said, "Uh, Lourdes . . . Uh . . . I'm going out Friday night. It's sort of for my birthday with a friend. And . . . Uh . . . I just wanted you to know so that you wouldn't wait dinner for me tomorrow night."

"You're going out with Marcela aren't you?" Her voice and face were steely.

"Yeah," he said unapologetically.

"Okay. Thanks for telling me."

Their body language did all the talking that evening. Lourdes could see Miguel was uncomfortable, but there seemed an excitement stirring inside of him, probably because he would have an evening to be young and have some fun.

Lourdes was uncomfortable, too, from sheer anger. Marcela was tantamount to a home-wrecker in her mind, even though she couldn't justify why.

For the first time in their unusual relationship, Lourdes felt strange sharing a bed with Miguel. She felt like sleeping on the couch, but they shared a room with Piper, and she didn't want to leave the baby. She thought about suggesting to Miguel that he sleep on the couch, but he hadn't done anything wrong. He had been a gentleman at every turn. Lourdes, irritated with herself for having this flood of angry emotions, rolled over and closed her eyes.

Friday morning started normally. Lourdes and Miguel were cordial to each other. Noticing that Miguel was taking a change of clothes with him to work, she ground her teeth into a stoic smile.

She wanted to go talk to Katie, but with Angela still sick she couldn't take Piper over. After lunch, her phone rang. Polly said, "Hello darlin', how are you?"

"I'm fine, thanks," lied Lourdes.

"Well, I have some news about a job prospect for you, and I'd like to drop by if you'll be home for a little while."

With a glimmer of hope breaking over the horizon she said, "Absolutely! Your timing is perfect!"

When Polly arrived at the pink house, Piper was dressed in a white shirt and a pink tutu. Polly cooed, "She is just such a little dolly baby."

"Thanks," Lourdes answered, aware that she sometimes forgot how cute of a baby Piper was in the midst of bad diapers, spit-up, and fussy nights.

"How are your days going?" asked Polly politely.

"They're all the same really," Lourdes answered, without wanting to say anything about how sorrowfully different was this day.

"You know, life is mundane and miraculous. We're only lucky enough to occasionally get a glimpse of the miraculous weaving through our day." Polly waved her hand with an air of magic.

"I don't think that miraculous day is today," Lourdes said with a downward sounding voice.

"Yes. Well. I have a friend, Pammy Penny, who has a friend named Jason, who owns a coffee shop in Memphis. He tends to hire college students, and he has a knack for hiring people who find themselves in a bit of a pickle. She gave me his phone number to give you. I think you'd like working there with people your own age."

Polly waited a moment, thinking Lourdes would say something. Lourdes sat without speaking so Polly leaned forward and asked, "Are you interested?"

"It just hit me that I'll need to hire a babysitter, and find a house, and I'm not sure how to get all of that done." Lourdes had coped with the unstable nature of her life by ignoring the obvious change ahead.

"Well, about the house, I asked Archie and he said that Miguel hadn't mentioned anything to him that he was going to leave at the end of the year. He was really shocked. He likes Miguel a great deal. Archie said that you could stay in the pink house for a while." Polly smiled, knowing that at least one fear had been allayed.

Lourdes started to cry. "I just feel so constantly overwhelmed. And that keeps me from doing anything at all."

"Don't you fret. Here is the phone number, I'll call Pammy to tell her that you'll be in touch soon."

The two women hugged while Polly reminded her to take things one step at a time.

As evening brought the setting sun, Miguel did not come home to hold the baby and talk about their day. Lourdes cooked herself a frozen pizza for dinner, now seeing only darkness out the kitchen window.

After Piper's bath and bottle, Lourdes put her in the crib. "It's just you and me. I guess I'll have to learn that loneliness is just an emotion for me to control." She nodded in agreement with herself, and patted the baby's back repeating, "Loneliness is just an emotion."

The house was quiet and still, which made every sound magnify to a terrifying level.

It was an excruciatingly long night. Every ten minutes she would look at the clock thinking that at least thirty minutes had passed. When she looked at the clock for the hundredth time and only two minutes had gone by, she decided not to look any more.

She had assumed Miguel would stay on his date with Marcela until midnight and be home around one in the morning. Miguel clearly had other ideas. After two o'clock, she wondered if he would be coming home that night at all. "Maybe he knew he was going to spend the night with her and that's why he took a change of clothes," Lourdes mumbled to herself, inwardly seething.

With time ticking by, she thought, 'This is too freaky. I'm going to need a roommate.' Her entire life she had shared a room with someone. Of course, no one had been the same kind of comfort that Miguel had been. It was sort of like living with a best friend. Actually, it was exactly like living with your best friend. "I'll need a roommate and a dog," she said, finishing her thought aloud.

At four o'clock she heard Miguel stumble in the front door. She didn't know what she would say to him and decided to feign sleeping. But Lourdes didn't need a game plan about what to say, he made no effort to communicate with her. Miguel loudly wobbled into the bathroom, and then she heard him fall onto the couch.

Infuriated, she muttered through clinched teeth, "He is drunk!"

Lourdes barely slept at all that night. The two hours of sleep she did grab were fitful, filled with even crazier than usual dreams.

At half-past six, Piper woke up. Lourdes wasn't sure if she should be quiet or try to make a lot of noise just to annoy Miguel. She couldn't stop herself from glaring at him lying on the couch, while only making the usual racket. Miguel didn't budge until mid-morning, after Piper had gone down for a nap.

"Good morning," Lourdes said, with no attempt at sounding pleasant.

"Huh?" Miguel's red eyes had a look of confusion.

"Did you have fun?!" Lourdes yelled, like it was a statement more than a question.

"I don't know. Uhhh, yeah. I guess, yeah." Miguel rubbed his head while he sat on the edge of the couch.

"So what did you do?" It was an interrogation.

"I think . . . I think . . . we went to a strip club." Miguel was rubbing his head as if he were trying to stimulate his brain cells. It was only this foggy haze that caused him to utter those words to Lourdes.

"You think? You THINK? You mean you don't KNOW if you went to a strip club?" yelled Lourdes.

A few brain cells must have cajoled awake because he realized he needed to stop talking. Excusing himself to the bathroom, he gave them both a moment to compose themselves.

Miguel emerged, clean, yet still scruffy, and sat down in the living room.

Lourdes, calmer, reminded herself again that Miguel didn't owe her anything, and this one year of being cared for was at its end. Not wanting to separate with hard feelings between them, she shut down the part of her that wanted Miguel to stay with her, choosing instead the logical thought that this was over and he was, as he had always been, free.

Purposefully walking to the couch and standing over him, she said, "I don't care where you went last night. You don't owe me any explanations. You don't owe me...," she trailed off while she thought how to finish the sentence. Looking him in the eyes, she said straightforwardly, "You don't owe me."

Lourdes, still facing the bleary-eyed Miguel, continued, "Polly and Katie are helping me, and I think I can stay in the pink house for a little bit, and maybe they've found me a job. Anyway, I've got to start planning my future."

Miguel wordlessly nodded, stood-up and walked into the bedroom to get some more sleep.

"That was rude," mumbled Lourdes. "Try to have a civil conversation and he walks off." Lourdes did a lot of mumbling that day – mainly to herself since she and Miguel had now had all the conversation they were going to have.

Sunday was spent silently smiling and nodding as they passed each other around the house.

Monday morning began quietly with Miguel giving Piper a gentle stroke on her head. He did not look at Lourdes on his way to the bathroom to get ready for work.

Lourdes knew since he tasted the wild, free life without obligation, he must regret the remaining time he had to spend with her and Piper.

Miguel's truck rumbled out of the driveway. Lourdes spent her day trying to convince herself that she didn't care, determined to complete this journey with Miguel with gratitude.

At five o'clock she heard the truck return, but there was also the sound of an extra truck pulling in the driveway behind Miguel. Peering out the window, she could see Archie Dallas. Both men were leaning against Miguel's work truck, not looking at each other, but talking – clearly engaged.

It was a beautiful day. Blue skies were blending into a soft, evening purple and the air was cool and dry.

Curiosity consumed Lourdes. She didn't want to just stand at the window, obviously watching, but she couldn't contain her perpetual peeking.

After what felt like an hour later, Mr. Dallas left. Lourdes, too inquisitive to be coy, asked Miguel, "What were you and Mr. Dallas talking about?"

Miguel simply answered, "Stuff." There was something about his demeanor that was different from the beleaguered Miguel of yesterday.

"Stuff?" asked Lourdes, her head leaning forward in anticipation of an explanation.

"Stuff. Guy stuff. That's all. What's for dinner?" His hand gave a waving, twitching motion.

"Ham and baked potatoes," she answered pointing to the oven. "Hey, listen, Miguel, I'm sorry for getting mad at you the other night. Whatever you do is your business, and I only want you to remember how thankful I am for everything you've done for me."

Her voice felt like it could choke-up. Swallowing hard, and with determined cheerfulness, she continued, "We need to figure out exactly what day you're moving and exactly how this is going to end."

"Sure. Yeah. Later." He spotted Piper, washed his hands and picked-up the baby.

Talking about their future plans turned out to be much later as two weeks passed without discussion from Miguel. Lourdes concluded that figuring this out with Miguel wasn't going to happen, so she would wait until he was gone to move forward. This brought a measure of peace as she had perfected the art of not making decisions. She still had her credit card with the five hundred dollar limit, which had been paid back to a zero balance long ago, and would need it after he was gone. Knowing Miguel would leave all the bills current, she would be starting fresh.

Thanksgiving was just around the corner. Katie and Tucker were going to spend the holiday in Little Rock with Cracker and Ginny. Jesse and the kids were going to visit Avy Faye's family, and even Big Momma was going with Polly and Peter to visit some friends in Memphis.

Lourdes had no experience in cooking a festive, holiday meal and happily agreed with Miguel's suggestion to buy a turkey with all the trimmings from a grocery store in Memphis. For twenty-nine dollars and ninety-nine cents they would have plenty of turkey, dressing, green beans and pumpkin pie. They placed their order to be picked up the day before Thanksgiving.

Late November was picture-perfect, exceptionally cool and crisp. Tennessee, it seemed, had actual seasons which was very different than her weather experience in central Texas, which was a melding of varying amounts of heat and humidity.

Miguel picked-up their feast in Memphis while running errands for Mr. Dallas, who had given Miguel a four-day weekend.

Lourdes noticed, without comment, that Marcela wasn't calling anymore and when Miguel went into Memphis he no longer had any interesting stories to share from Marcela. Maybe he was just being kind. Lourdes didn't ask.

Lourdes had called about the job at the coffee shop, and she felt confident the welcoming voice on the other end of the phone would hire her when the time came.

She endlessly thought about what would happen to her after Christmas, very few of her scenarios gave her much cheer because her imagination was much more adept at imagining the worst.

Lourdes didn't feel lovable. She didn't feel beautiful. She had a baby to take care of, which was a very different job than she thought it would be. Babies were work. Being a mom wasn't a Monday through Friday, eight to five, with an hour for lunch, job with sick days and paid vacations. It's an all day, every day, all the time, volunteer position, where your little patron screams at you without apology. Piper didn't love her unconditionally, Piper unconditionally required her assistance.

Although she loved Piper, the thought of allowing Roy and Miguel's parents to raise her incessantly crept into her thoughts as the most loving option for this precious baby. She could stay in Kingsville while Miguel would be in Texas to watch over Piper with his parents.

She darkly wondered if she was very much different than her own mother, who was incapable of providing a life for her baby. "No," she would tell herself. "Aunt Connie never wanted me, but Miguel's parents want Piper. And," she encouraged herself, "I'll be a part of her life. I'll make sure she always knows I love her and only wanted the best for her." With a pathetic smile, she reminded herself that Miguel would always be there for Piper, and no one was better than him.

The Thanksgiving turkey dinner was moderately better than adequate but the football was good. Miguel liked that Lourdes enjoyed football - one of the perks of being with a girl from Texas.

They had fun together, nibbling and cheering throughout a lazy, overcast day.

"You'll never believe what happened to Jane when they were at *Target*," Lourdes said to Miguel, while she handed him more dip for his chips. Acting out the story, in a most animated way, she said, "Her middle son had a loose tooth; and when Jane turned around to look at something - well, her purse swung just so - and it hit him in the mouth! His tooth went flying out!

And then, after she got the bleeding to stop, she bent down to look for it but couldn't find the tooth. But she did find a pair of shoes that she liked, so she picked them up to take to the check out . . . And then . . . when they were walking to the check out - the little one started crying. She picked him up, *and he threw up* inside the box with the new pair of shoes.

I mean, REALLY. You just can't make this stuff up. Nobody has enough imagination to invent a story like that!"

Miguel, who enjoyed her spirited storytelling, mused, "I wonder what kind of crazy things Piper is going to get into." Then asked what Jane did with the shoes.

Lourdes said, "She bought them and threw them away!"

The day ended just as happily as it began.

Polly came back from her Thanksgiving dinner, calling Lourdes with news. Her friend at the coffee shop said they were in need of holiday help, and they were interested in Lourdes starting soon.

Caught off guard, Lourdes said, "Wow . . . I . . . I don't know what to say."

Polly answered, "I'll tell you what to say...say that you'll make a bee-line to Memphis! Katie and I will take care of Piper while you go!"

Feeling like her throat could close from agony, Lourdes ended the phone call with a guttural, "Thanks."

Her unsaid thoughts of Piper moving with Miguel stopped her as she envisioned buckling Piper into her car seat - and watching them drive away.

Would she run after them, begging to go live with his parents, too? How would she feel watching the next Marcela in Miguel's life? Or did she really want to raise Piper in poverty when the baby had a chance at something better?

The heart-wrenching fact was the time had come to decide. What would become of Piper?

WHAT LOVE MEANT

E li handed them the bulletin at King's Community Church say-ing, "It will be a warm and mild start to the week, but changes are ahead."

Jesse walked up to say hello to Lourdes, Miguel and Piper, who was sleeping in her baby carrier. "Did you have a good Thanksgiving?" he asked.

"Yup," answered Miguel. "We watched a lot of football and ate a turkey dinner we picked up from the grocery store. The food was pretty good, but I think I can bake a better pumpkin pie, except my pie is always runny in the middle, but it tastes all right." Miguel added the last part about the pie mainly as a comment to himself. "And you?" he asked Jesse.

"Pretty good. We went to see Avy's brother and his family. It feels like the first of every holiday without her is going to be un-bearable," Jesse's face was careworn as his voice trailed off.

Wandering toward his dad, Eli stopped and put his arms around his father's waist in a steadying hug. Jesse hugged him and summoning courage, brightly said, "Then we came home and put up the Christmas tree!"

Eli explained, "Yeah. We put up the tree the Saturday after Thanksgiving, and then we put up a tent in the living room, and we slept there all night. It was really cool because we left the lights twinkling all night long."

Lourdes and Miguel didn't know what to say. They stood among this small circle of hurting souls, each with a painful smile. Miguel put his hand on top of Eli's head and said, "Maybe I should put up a tree, too."

Miguel's suggestion couldn't have shocked Lourdes more. She said, "A tree? We don't even have any ornaments or decorations."

Angela joined the huddled group, and also put her arms around her father's waist. "We can make you ornaments," she said.

Jesse looked lovingly at his children. "They make the best ornaments in the world! Give them popsicle sticks, glitter, construction paper and glue, and they'll give you a masterpiece!" Then looking back up at Miguel he said, "I've seen Christmas tree lots around Memphis that have those small Charlie Brown trees for ten bucks, and it wouldn't take many ornaments to decorate those."

"Okay!" Miguel answered, which ended the conversation since Sister Hessie had started playing the first hymn.

Before they could reach their appointed pew, Polly breezed by Lourdes and asked if she had called the coffee shop.

Miguel looked quizzically at Lourdes, who shook her head but didn't explain.

Eli was right, the weather changed quickly. The cool rains of December kept the residents of the pink house from getting a tree for the next week.

The next Sunday, the little family skipped church and packed-up Piper to go buy her first Christmas tree. Miguel was certain that it being a small tree, it could ride in the trunk of his car travelling with its happy, holiday, treetop poking out.

Twenty dollars later they had a scraggly tree, vanilla Cokes, burgers and fries, and were on their way back to the pink house.

"Lourdes, I've been thinking," Miguel's voice was serious and firm.

It had been such a lovely afternoon. But now a wave of dread washed over Lourdes. There was a hint of finality in Miguel's voice. It dawned on Lourdes that he wanted to have this nice moment to soften her disappointment when he described how they would sever ties with each other. She bit her lower lip in anticipation and stared ahead.

Every time Lourdes tried to decide if Piper should stay with her and forge an unknown, poverty-filled life or go with Miguel's parents, a heartbroken Lourdes felt physically sick.

Even though Lourdes wanted to mentally check out of the conversation, Miguel kept talking. This was it. No more putting off the inevitable.

"Actually, it started with Mr. Dallas. A couple of weeks ago, he wanted to talk to me about you staying in the pink house, and he wondered why I hadn't told him myself that I was leaving," Miguel said.

Nervously, Lourdes babbled, "Well, I needed to find a place to stay, and a job, and Polly was just trying to help." Calming herself she added, "And, well, I'm happy here. I have help and support. I can't imagine having to go back to my aunt's house . . . well, actually I can't go back there. I'm just trying to figure out what's best for Piper and, truly, I'm happy here, but I do want Piper to be properly cared for . . ."

Miguel didn't let her finish, "Lourdes, I'm happy here, too. I think the reason I didn't tell Mr. Dallas that I was going home was because I didn't really want to go. But I didn't feel like it was right to stay here, either.

Mr. Dallas asked me why it wouldn't be right, and I told him, well, I told him that . . ." Miguel was still hesitant, the words clogging his vocal cords.

Straightening up to sit a little higher in his seat, he continued, "I told him that since you had been with my brother I didn't think it would be right to be with you.

Mr. Dallas told me that the Bible talks about something called a 'kinsman-redeemer' where it was a privilege and a responsibility to care for the family of a brother who passed away."

There was that word - responsible. Responsible for her? Before Miguel could say anymore, something new bloomed inside of Lourdes. Never again would she feel she was someone's responsibility. A lovely thought sprouted that she was enough - just as she was. She was loved by God - just as she was. She would find God's plan for her life – just as she was.

An inner strength must have been growing, unseen, like a tiny flower breaking through the concrete crack in the sidewalk.

Confidently, Lourdes said, "Miguel," stopping her sentence, then starting again with a stronger voice, "Miguel, if you don't want to be here, well, I don't want you here. I mean, I've appreciated *EVERYTHING* that you've done for me. Seriously, I don't know what would have happened if you hadn't given up your past year to help me."

There was a quiet pause before she continued, "My whole life someone has taken care of me out of obligation." Her voice was shaky, but she didn't cry. "That stops today. I don't want any person in my life to be there because they feel obligated."

Voicing her thoughts, punctuating every word, she said, "*Never* again will I be someone else's *responsibility.*"

"No, no. I mean, no. That's not what I'm saying at all." Miguel took his eyes off the road, looked at Lourdes, and said, "I'm happy here. Happy with you. Happy with Piper. Happy with my job. This should have been the worst year of my life after Roy died, and instead it was hard - but in a good way. Lourdes this has been the best year of my life. I don't want things to change.

Well, I do want things to change. I'd like to . . . I'd like to take care of you as my wife."

"Miguel, you're already taking care of me. Do you mean you want to stay in Kingsville?" Lourdes asked, not comprehending his point.

"Not exactly." His eyes were back on the road. Looking at the familiar scenery flashing by must have seemed easier than facing Lourdes. "I'd like for you and I to be married in every way, like a real couple."

It was a simple statement that Lourdes couldn't even begin to believe. She felt plain and frumpy. Her post-baby tummy slightly drooped over the buckled seat belt. He had seen her naked, but it was in the midst of a messy childbirth. They had slept in the same bed, but it was comforting and comfortable to have him there, and nothing else.

Married in every way - what did he mean? While processing her thoughts, she looked out the window away from Miguel. Lourdes heard him clear his throat, seeming nervous.

"Lourdes," he said while simultaneously she said, "Miguel."

It was Lourdes who continued with a furrowed brow. "Miguel, what do you want from me?"

"I want . . . I want . . . us to be a couple . . . no . . . a family. I want you and I to figure out where we go from here, together. I like living with you. I like . . ." Miguel was not good at expressing himself even under normal circumstances.

Lourdes had figured out, a long time ago, that when they went to a fast food restaurant they needed to order inside, because ordering into an outdoor microphone somehow created a magnetic brain signal that jammed his ability to speak clearly.

Smiling at that thought, she simply asked Miguel, "Why? You're not in love with me."

"Yes, Lourdes, I think I am." He took his eyes off the road only to see Lourdes's stunned expression.

The road between Memphis and Kingsville continued whizzing by - the overgrown thickets with old fence posts, the pastures and the trees.

Still not believing what she had just heard, she could barely dare to think that Miguel – the nicest, kindest, most helpful person she had ever met - thought he loved her.

"Miguel, you're the best man I've ever known. I mean . . . I can't even imagine this is true!" Lourdes's hands were waving wildly as if to punctuate her sentences. "When Marcela kept calling you and you stayed out the night with her . . . I tried hard not to be furious."

"Yeah," Miguel answered with a solemn voice. "Well, the morning after our date, I looked in the mirror, and it was like Roy was looking back at me."

Lourdes wondered if the timeworn notion was true. Miguel didn't like what he saw in the mirror behind the dull vantage point of his bloodshot eyes.

Miguel's voice sounded pained as he said, "I'd seen him look like that a thousand times. I always thought he looked like he'd been having fun, partying with everybody. I didn't know that behind that face was a booming headache and fuzzy memories of the night before. Roy always laughed it off.

And, well, it was like . . . he was trying to tell me something . . . like he wanted to save my life, and not end up like him."

Miguel looked grieved talking about Roy, but continued, saying, "I've seen lots of girls like Marcela. I thought maybe that's what I wanted – just fun, goofing around. Funny thing is, I think I had more fun playing Bunco at Katie's house than going out with Marcela. I can't be totally sure I didn't have as much fun, though, because I really don't remember everything."

His nose let out a little sniff while his lips curved up in a smile. "But I do know I feel better about myself working for Mr. Dallas, and where I'm going when I'm with you . . . you . . . your crazy dreams . . . you little weirdo."

Miguel looked at Lourdes, who was looking back at him, and then he sweetly and gently patted her knee. "Being with you is a privilege - not a responsibility."

Lourdes felt loved. If an emotion ever became a physical feeling it was in that moment, in that car, with a sleeping baby in her car seat, and a twig of a Christmas tree peeking out the trunk.

Lourdes felt loved.

With newfound joy, she managed to say, "I love you, too. Every day when I hear your rumbling truck pull into the driveway, my heart gives a little jump. I just never thought you'd feel that way about me," she finished with quiet elation.

She wiped the tears from her face, and he held her soppy hand the rest of the way home. It was a joyful ride, the happiest ever. She was going home to the pink house with her family - *her* real family.

The weighty, cumbersome burden that was her constant companion lifted in an instant. The result was almost physical as she took maybe the first, real, deep-cleansing breath of her life.

"But I want to have a real wedding," she said when they were almost home. "In Las Vegas it was Roy that I was marrying, in my mind, and now I want it to be really you and really me."

Surprisingly, Miguel agreed. "All right. We can do it a couple of days before Christmas like before."

"No. No, not on the twenty-third," Lourdes said with her forehead crinkled. A mere moment later she softly said, "Christmas Eve. Christmas Eve, let's do it then."

Miguel nodded his approval.

At the pink house, arranging the child-made ornaments from Angela and Eli, with lots of string lights, they made the most radiant tree Lourdes had ever seen.

That night as the little family lay in their bedroom, Lourdes felt self-conscious. Just the night before she had gotten into her pajamas, chatted for a moment, and nodded off to sleep. Tonight, Lourdes wondered how she looked, what Miguel was thinking, what Miguel would be expecting. Miguel wore his white undershirt and blue gym shorts. They chatted for a moment then he touched her arm, squeezed her hand, and rolled over.

The next morning, Miguel went to work, and Lourdes took Piper over to Katie's house. Happy to see the friendly front doors of Safehaven, she had a zillion thoughts floating through her brain that needed a voice.

She needed the advice of the one person whose wisdom she trusted - Katie.

Lourdes and Katie sat in the comfortable squishy chairs in the great room, while Piper played in her bouncer. Unable to bind her exuberance, Lourdes said, "Miguel thinks he wants us to be married, like, for real. He wants to have a real ceremony and try this for real. What do you think?"

With her eyes widened, Katie answered, "Wow! Oh my goodness! You and Miguel making a go of it, huh?"

Lourdes and Katie exchanged easy smiles.

"I think I do love him. I'm just not really sure I know what love means." A vulnerable tone mingled in the joy of Lourdes's voice.

Lourdes knew Katie understood everything that led to this point - there hadn't been much opportunity for feeling safe and loved in relationships.

"Well," Katie started with a click of her tongue. "I think these days when people say they're 'in love,' what they're really saying is their personalities get on well with each other. And when people say they've 'fallen out of love' with each other, what they really mean is their personalities collide more than they blend.

I've watched you and Miguel this past year. You're both such kind-hearted souls." Katie leaned toward Lourdes and gave her knee a pat. "And I can see you two getting along really well through life."

Lourdes remained silent so Katie continued, "The romantic feelings people think are love are really fun, intimate moments that flit through our seasons depending on your day . . . or his day, or . . . just circumstances really. As much as we do need all of that, well, love is much more solid."

Piper kicked something in her bouncer, which made a jingly sound, causing a pause in the moment.

Katie used the instant to collect her thoughts. "Love is like . . . well, you're telling Miguel - and he is telling you - that you're choosing to elevate each other to give the best of yourselves. At least that should be the goal," Katie finished, laughing.

Lourdes simply looked at Katie, and still didn't have a comment, so Katie continued, "But you already know what love is. It's when you get up in the middle of the night to take care of Piper, while she is not only ungrateful - she screams so you'll give her better service!

Love was when Jesse comforted and cared for Avy Faye until her dying day, giving her confidence that he would always take care of their children, even saying that they'd be okay - knowing nothing was okay.

Love was when Avy knew she was dying - and she bravely faced it so it wouldn't be any harder on her family than it already was."

Looking around at her lovely home, Katie said, "Love was Tucker going off to work in another country to provide for us when our business failed. Love was when I let him do it and lived like a vagabond while he was gone."

Katie had never before tried to give a concise answer about how to define love. Her forehead crinkled as if to squeeze out every drop of wisdom, finishing with, "Love is the extraordinary giving of yourself. And when two people trade that level of care... it is romantically life-enhancing."

There was a moment in the room when Lourdes could feel her mood shift.

"What if it's all a mistake? What if he leaves me?" Lourdes looked so deeply into Katie's eyes, it was as if to divine the future.

"All any of us can do . . . me . . . you . . . anyone," Katie answered, "is to make the best prayerful decision we can with the information we have.

And then you have to live forward-looking. If you live looking back, wondering if you got it wrong, you'll miss all the lovely scenery the Lord has for today."

Lourdes didn't cry, but with a shaky voice said, "But what if he leaves me?"

It was a difficult question because Katie had friends who had endured that very situation.

"Divorce isn't easy. I have friends who are divorced. Christian families experience life just like everyone else. But what I **know** to be true is they've lived to see God and His goodness at work blessing them."

Katie looked into the depth of Lourdes's pain so profoundly that Lourdes could feel it. Katie concisely said, "God's love for *YOU* will never fail.

You are not now – and you never will be - a beggar for love."

Realizing she had been leaning forward with such intensity she was almost doubled over, Lourdes relaxed, easing back into the cushions.

With a smile and a nod of her head, Lourdes said, "I do love Miguel. He is funny and helpful, and when I hear his truck chugging home, and hear his shoes crunching on the pebbles in the driveway, I feel happy. And he does . . . he gives so generously of himself to me every day."

Katie grinned and said, "You will always have to hold onto that thought, because I can almost *guarantee* you that some days you will feel really annoyed with him - he *will* be on the naughty list - and remembering those moments are quite helpful."

As the concerns Lourdes had been carrying in her heart began to be replaced with hope, she looked at Katie with small tears popping out of her eyes like translucent pearls. She said, "You've changed my life. I don't know what would have happened to me if you hadn't cared about me."

Unable to find the right words, Katie silently hugged Lourdes.

Wiping tears with her sleeve, Lourdes noticed the battery-powered wreath above the fireplace, and recalled it was merely one Christmas ago she and Miguel had walked through the red doors of Safehaven. She had been adrift in every definition of the word.

A joyful giggle choked out the last tear. "Okay. Yeah," was all Lourdes said as she packed-up Piper to go home to the pink house.

Later that evening, Lourdes heard Miguel's truck pulling into the driveway. He opened the door, they smiled at each other, just like they had done for these many months past, but this time with a secret excitement.

Piper fussed and kicked while she sat in her bouncer during supper. Lourdes and Miguel made their plans for a Christmas Eve wedding. The lights from the Christmas tree reflected the sparkle in the eyes of the people who lived in the pink house.

The Christmas Eve sun rose bright and cheery. The mild temperatures were perfect for an outdoor wedding in the garden at Safehaven.

Waiting for them were the same folks who had waited for them on Christmas Eve last: Katie and Tucker; Katie's parents, Cracker and Ginny Philpott; Katie's daughter, Julie, with Luke and baby Caleb.

Missing would be sweet, gentle Avy Faye. But Jesse and the children were coming to witness the union. Pastor Aaron and his wife, Mary Frances, would be performing the ceremony.

Mr. Archie Dallas would be attending, which they all knew was an honor since he seldom ventured to parties of any kind.

Lourdes planned on wearing a dress she had worn many times before, but her first wedding gift was a wedding dress that Julie brought for her.

A look of astonishment crossed Lourdes's face when she opened the gift box containing the lacy, fanciful, antique white dress. "It's so beautiful! I can't even begin to say thank-you enough!"

"Well, mom told me about the ceremony, and I thought that you'd look really pretty in this dress. I hope it fits all right. Honestly, it was my favorite gift I shopped for this Christmas," Julie said as she smiled happily.

"And," Julie said when Ginny walked into the conversation, "she paid for the dress," pointing to her grandmother.

"Oh, that was supposed to be between you and I." Ginny lovingly hugged Julie, and turning to Lourdes, squeezed her, saying, "My prayers for a blessed future."

Thanking both of them for their generosity, Lourdes felt like a fairy tale princess.

Miguel had borrowed a black suit from their friend Jane's husband, Bob. Piper wore a velvety red dress with lace along the hem, white tights and shiny black shoes. A big white bow contrasted with her jet black hair.

They all walked out into the garden, where white twinkle lights wrapped around the trees and draped overhead, creating a canopy of lights, which sparkled like well-wishes from hundreds of Christmas stars.

It was six in the evening, and the setting sun had left behind a watercolor glow as a wedding gift. It was a small intimate wedding, in a beautiful garden, filled with lovely people, who surrounded Lourdes and Miguel with their love.

With a rocking motion, Katie held Piper, who had chosen this moment to have a minor fuss fit. Julie stood beside her mother, holding Caleb, who was now a two-year-old. In order to assure that

Caleb behaved through the ceremony, he was munching from a baggie filled with cereal.

Lourdes carried a bouquet of white daisies with yellow centers, and walked to Miguel's side as they faced Pastor Aaron. He smiled at them and began, "I remember last year seeing you at our Christmas program. Remember how we raced through it so we could all be home before the storm?"

Everyone nodded.

Continuing, he said, "It's impossible to see the unseen spirit realm. It's shrouded from our view, and the evidence of its involvement gets tossed in with the chaos and clutter of our daily life.

Today, I believe we have the evidence of how our steps are ordered by the Lord. Without the hardships that Tucker and Katie endured with their business closing, they wouldn't have known loss, only to rebuild their lives here in Kingsville, operating this wonderful bed and breakfast.

And," Pastor Aaron said with his broad grin, "I understand without Miguel stopping by the side of the road to help a truck driver in need, Lourdes wouldn't have gotten out of her car, only to meet a woman who had a magazine advertising this place.

We know the rest of the story that followed this God-ordained meeting.

God has a plan. God sends his angels to whisper hints of opportunity to point us in the right direction.

Sometimes they whisper their instructions to the deep part of our souls. And sometimes . . . I think they use travel magazines."

Everyone chuckled.

"All I know - is that we are all so very glad, so very blessed, those steps brought Lourdes, Miguel, and Piper to us."

The small gallery murmured agreement.

Pastor Aaron waited a moment and continued, "Lourdes and Miguel, as encouragers to each other, you can find that path toward the highest and best.

But let me tell you a secret about how you live happily ever after. You live happily ever after . . . one imperfect day at a time."

Katie smiled and looked at Tucker, as they both nodded in agreement.

Lourdes and Miguel repeated their vows to each other underneath the cascading shower of lights. Through the window Lourdes noticed the dazzling Christmas tree inside of Safehaven - along with a smoldering fire in the fireplace which gave off a fuzzy glow. No wedding could have been more romantic.

The only sound in the still air was Caleb crunching his cereal.

Miguel slipped back onto Lourdes's finger the small silver ring he had purchased at the pawn shop one year ago. It was a quick ceremony ending with a kiss – a real kiss this time – with a real bride and groom, filled with real love.

Jesse, who was experiencing his first Christmas without his wife, shook Miguel's hand, hugged him, and said, "Cherish your wife . . . just . . . always cherish your wife."

Soon afterwards, they all drove to King's Community Church, anticipating the Christmas program and desserts.

The final surprise of the evening was the reception the women of King's Community Church planned for Lourdes and Miguel.

Although they still had Christmas tree shaped cookies, Jane had made a three-tiered wedding cake, turning an after-Christmas-program-party into an enjoyable, memorable wedding reception.

Polly organized everyone to make sure Lourdes and Miguel felt a community of love. Lourdes gushed with gratitude.

That night, Katie and Tucker took care of Piper so Lourdes and Miguel could have the night alone at the pink house. There was no money for a honeymoon, but hopefully, there would be time and resources for that later.

They didn't care.

The next morning, Lourdes woke up and said, "I had the craziest dream last night. I dreamed I was friends with this girl on a TV show I like. On the show, she's my age, but in the dream, she was like seventy years old. Then she said she wanted to go to Cozumel . . ."

Miguel nodded and grinned. "Come on. I think you have a present under the tree.

EPILOGUE
FIVE YEARS ON

Miguel was torn - pay attention to the person on the phone, who he was trying to give his address to - or Lourdes, who was loudly telling him, "Well, just tell them we live in Big Momma's old house. Surely they know where that is!"

Walking back into the bedroom, she mumbled, "Everybody knows where we live."

Miguel, finishing the phone call, asked Lourdes, "Why didn't you just tell me what you got? I could've just picked it up."

Running late and exasperated, Lourdes said, "Because Hessie said the quilt wasn't quite finished, and when it was finished they'd bring it to her, and then she would have someone bring it to me."

Lourdes and Miguel had lived quite happily in Big Momma's house for the past three years. After Big Momma passed on, they bought her house, and worked – as money allowed – updating it to become their very own home, always happy when they stumbled upon something of Big Momma's that had been lost to time.

Piper skipped into the room wearing a lime-green, smocked dress with a pink watermelon stitched on the front. "Will Angela be there?" she asked.

"I'm sure she will, sweetheart," Lourdes answered, stroking Piper's thick dark hair as she walked by.

"Will the new baby be there?" wondered Piper.

"No. The party is for us to bring presents for the new baby, so when the baby is born, and comes home with Mr. Jesse and Miss Michelle, they'll have lots of things to take care of the baby with."

"That reminds me," Miguel said, looking at Lourdes, "Jesse told me he is going to take a full month off when the baby is born so we can't carpool that month."

Astonished, Lourdes said, "A month? It's great your company will let him do that. Do you remember how hard it was when Piper was born?

If he can take a full month off, then maybe he won't feel so sleep-deprived. I mean, he isn't as young as he used to be! Imagine - Eli is barely a teenager and they're going to have a baby!"

"Yeah," said Miguel, "and remind me to say something to Eli about being a weatherman intern this summer."

"It's not really a true internship. I mean, he's too young," Lourdes said, laughing, "but he's so excited, you'd think he was going to be on TV handing out bulletins - along with a weather report - to the whole city of Memphis!"

Quietly thinking of Avy Faye, Lourdes said something she had been tossing around in her mind. "I'm glad Jesse found Michelle. She is so perfect for him! And Eli and Angela love her so much.

I think Avy would be happy about it all, too. In heaven, I think they'll all be great friends. I'm sure because Avy always, only, wanted them to be cared for and happy....But I wish Avy was still here," she ended, almost in a whisper.

Saying out loud what she had been pondering seemed to relieve her slightly muddled emotions. Wishing she could tell Avy things had turned out well for everyone brought a comfort to her soul.

Glancing at the clock by her bed, she said, "If someone doesn't bring the quilt fast, maybe I can just run to the Mercantile and pick out something else."

Miguel added, "You know, I still can't believe that it was Clayton Hobbs that lowered the flag to half-staff the day of Avy's funeral."

"I know!" Lourdes answered. "After he died, if Hessie hadn't found the note he wrote no one would ever have known. I guess Avy had a way of bringing out the best in everybody.

As mean as it sounds though," Lourdes breathed, "I like shopping at the Mercantile so much more now that he's not there."

The knock on the front door summoned Piper, who took the package containing the baby quilt already beautifully wrapped in a gift bag.

The little family hopped into their car and drove past the pink house toward Safehaven.

Lourdes didn't always notice the pink house anymore, but today, possibly because she had thought of Avy Faye, she glanced over at it and smiled, fondly remembering.

Remembering the rumbling truck - with *Archie Dallas Farms* written in faded letters...remembering how hot or how cold the house felt forced them to cram into one room . . . remembering how bitterly alone she felt when she arrived in Kingsville...remembering the day-by-day process of falling in love with Miguel.

She smiled, remembering.

The parking pad in front of Safehaven Bed and Breakfast was already full. Miguel parked along the side of the road, and together they walked up the long driveway.

Walking too slowly for her liking, and thinking of the promised cake inside, Piper tugged on Miguel's hand saying, "Come on, Daddy!"

The first to greet them was Angela, who thought of Piper as her personal baby doll.

For a moment, Lourdes's mind returned to the first time she entered the red doors of Safehaven. It had been filled with talking, laughing people, just like it was today. Previously they were unknown strangers, but today they were welcoming friends.

Lourdes, kindled by the remembrance of the course she had travelled, glowingly looked at Miguel, squeezed his hand, and thought it was true what she had been told at their wedding . . .

They were all living happily-ever-after . . . one imperfect day at a time.